"You're having my baby, Angela."

"That didn't seem to matter to you when I told you," she reminded Clint.

"That was then. This is now," he declared. "I've been trying to catch up with you since the day you left."

"Why?"

"Because no child of mine is going to grow up without a father," he said simply, his gaze locked with hers. A shudder seemed to wash over her, even as a spark of pure defiance lit her eyes.

"It's not your decision," she retorted.

"Yes," Clint said softly. "It is. As of this minute, I'm making it mine."

Dear Reader,

The holiday season has arrived—and we have some dazzling titles for the month of December!

This month, the always-delightful Joan Elliott Pickart brings you our THAT'S MY BABY! title. *Texas Baby* is the final book in her FAMILY MEN cross-line series with Desire, and spins the heartwarming tale of a fortysomething heroine who rediscovers the joy of motherhood when she adopts a precious baby girl. Except the dashing man of her dreams has no intention of playing daddy again....

And baby fever doesn't stop there. Don't miss *The Littlest Angel* by Sherryl Woods, an emotional reunion romance—and the first of her AND BABY MAKES THREE: THE NEXT GENERATION miniseries. Passion flares between a disgruntled cowboy and a tough lady cop in *The Cop and the Cradle* by Suzannah Davis—book two in the SWITCHED AT BIRTH miniseries.

For those of you who revel in holiday miracles, be sure to check out *Christmas Magic* by Andrea Edwards. This humorous romance features a cat-toting heroine who transforms a former Mr. Scrooge into a true believer—and captures his heart in the process.

Also this month, *The Millionaire's Baby* by Phyllis Halldorson is an absorbing amnesia story that's filled with love, turmoil and a possible second chance at happiness. Finally, long-buried feelings resurface when a heroine returns to unite her former lover with the son he'd never known in *Second Chance Dad* by Angela Benson.

All of us here at Silhouette wish you a joyous holiday season!

Sincerely,

Tara Gavin,
Senior Editor

Please address questions and book requests to:
Silhouette Reader Service
U.S.: 3010 Walden Ave., P.O. Box 1325, Buffalo, NY 14269
Canadian: P.O. Box 609, Fort Erie, Ont. L2A 5X3

SHERRYL WOODS

THE LITTLEST ANGEL

Published by Silhouette Books

America's Publisher of Contemporary Romance

SILHOUETTE BOOKS

ISBN 0-373-24142-9

THE LITTLEST ANGEL

Books by Sherryl Woods

Silhouette Special Edition

Safe Harbor #425
Never Let Go #446
Edge of Forever #484
In Too Deep #522
Miss Liz's Passion #573
Tea and Destiny #595
My Dearest Cal #669
Joshua and the Cowgirl #713
*Love #769
*Honor #775
*Cherish #781
*Kate's Vow #823
*A Daring Vow #855
*A Vow To Love #885
The Parson's Waiting #907
One Step Away #927
Riley's Sleeping Beauty #961
†Finally a Bride #987
‡A Christmas Blessing #1001
‡Natural Born Daddy #1007
‡The Cowboy and His Baby #1009
*‡The Rancher and His Unexpected
  Daughter* #1016
**A Ranch for Sara #1083
**Ashley's Rebel #1087
**Danielle's Daddy Factor #1094
††The Littlest Angel #1142

Silhouette Desire

Not at Eight, Darling #309
Yesterday's Love #329
Come Fly with Me #345
A Gift of Love #375
Can't Say No #431
Heartland #472
One Touch of Moondust #521
Next Time...Forever #601
Fever Pitch #620
Dream Mender #708

Silhouette Books

*Silhouette Summer Sizzlers
1990 "A Bridge to Dreams"*

*Vows
†Always a Bridesmaid!
‡And Baby Makes Three
**The Bridal Path
††And Baby Makes Three:
    The Next Generation

SHERRYL WOODS

lives by the ocean, which, she says, provides daily inspiration for the romance in her soul. She further explains that her years as a television critic taught her about steamy plots and humor; her years as a travel editor took her to exotic locations; and her years as a crummy weekend tennis player taught her to stick with what she enjoyed most—writing. "What better way is there," Sherryl asks, "to combine all that experience than by creating romantic stories?" Sherryl loves to hear from her readers. You may write to her at P.O. Box 490326, Key Biscayne, FL 33149. A self-addressed, stamped envelope is appreciated for a reply.

ADAMS FAMILY TREE

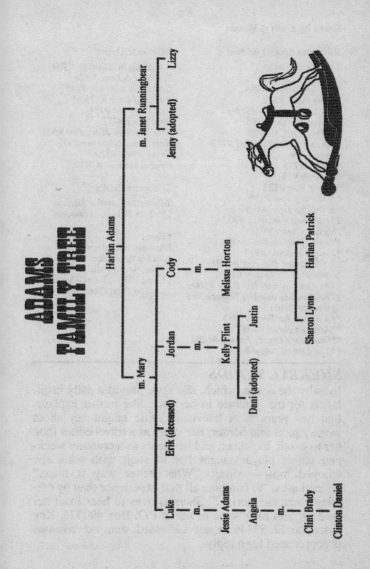

Harlan Adams

m. Mary — Harlan Adams — m. Janet Runningbear

m. Mary branch:
- Luke
- Erik (deceased)
- Jordan
- Cody

m. Janet Runningbear branch:
- Jenny (adopted)
- Lizzy

Luke m. Jessie Adams
- Angela
- Clint Brady
- Clinton Daniel

Jordan m. Kelly Flint
- Dani (adopted)
- Justin

Cody m. Melissa Horton
- Sharon Lynn
- Harlan Patrick

Chapter One

Angela hadn't wanted to come home like this, with her belly the size of two watermelons, and not one single proud accomplishment she could claim. She'd always meant her return to be triumphant, proof that she could succeed on her own without relying on the Adams name that meant so much in one little corner of West Texas. She'd envisioned a banner across the porch and a barbecue in her honor in the backyard and her name in lights, if Grandpa Harlan had his way.

Instead, it was the dead of night and no one even knew she was coming. Until she'd driven down the last stretch of deserted highway, anticipation mounting with every mile, she hadn't known for sure herself if she would have the courage to face her family. The car had settled that for her. It had conked out less than a mile from home. She sat in the rapidly chilling air and shivered, wondering if fate was on her side this time or just out to humiliate her further.

Home. The word had always conjured up a barrage of images for her, some good, some bad. Over the last six years the bad ones had faded until only the special memories remained. With her birthday tomorrow and Christmas just a few days away, it was no surprise that it was the holiday memories that came back to her now in a flood.

The celebrations always began early and lasted through New Year's, with everyone—aunts, uncles, cousins—traipsing from home to home for one party or another, but always, *always* ending up at White Pines. Grandpa Harlan insisted on it. He claimed he could spoil his grandkids rotten in his own home on Christmas Day if he chose to, while anywhere else he might have to show some restraint.

Rather than feeling deprived that her birthday was so close to Christmas, Angela had always felt as if all of the holiday trimmings made the day more special than it would have been at any other time of the year. Other kids got cakes and a single party. Angela's celebration included a huge tree, blinking colored lights, endless music and nonstop parties that went on for days.

She'd missed that while she was away, missed it when she'd noted the occasion all alone in a college rooming house already deserted by students who'd headed home for the holidays. Last year she'd almost forgotten it herself. She was too caught up in love, too excited about sharing her first Christmas with a man who really mattered to her.

Now, though, the memories were as vivid as if she'd never left. Even from her stalled car way out here on a lonely Texas highway she imagined she could see the lights twinkling on the ceiling-scraping Christmas tree, smell the aroma of Consuela's fresh-baked sugar cookies and bread mingling with the scent of fresh-cut pine. She could almost hear the sound of carols being played at full volume, while her dad chided her mom that she was going to deafen all of them.

She sighed as she remembered the angel of shimmering gold that was ceremoniously placed on top of the tree each and every year and the pride she'd felt when that duty had been given to her. At five she'd been too small to reach the top, so her father had hoisted her up on his broad shoulders so she could settle that frothy angel onto the tree's highest branch. Then and only then, in a room that had been darkened for the ceremony, did they switch on the lights, always too many of them, always so magical that she and her mom had gasped with delight, while her dad had grinned tolerantly. The same ceremony had been repeated at White Pines, where as the oldest grandchild she'd always been the one who'd put the angel on her grandfather's tree.

So many wonderful traditions, she thought now. How could she have run away from all the warmth and love in that house? she wondered in retrospect.

Rebellion, pure and simple. She had chafed at all the bright expectations and what she now suspected had been imagined pressures. Like all families, hers had only wanted what was best for her.

It was just that the Adams men, particularly Luke and her grandfather, had a tendency to think they were the only ones who knew what was best. No two men on earth could be more mule-headed once they'd charted a course of action, for themselves or someone they loved.

Ironically, they had rarely agreed on what that course should be. One plan would have been hard enough to fight, but two were impossible. Angela had wanted to decide her future for herself, and leaving—choosing a college far from Texas where the Adams influence didn't reach—had been the only way she'd seen to do it. She'd limited contact to occasional calls, an infrequent e-mail to her computer-literate father.

Now, with snow falling in fat, wet clumps and the roads turning into hazardous sheets of ice, she sat in her idled clunker of a car less than a mile from home and wondered if anything else could possibly go wrong. Even as the thought crossed her mind, she glanced quickly heavenward.

"Not that I'm tempting fate, You understand," she said wearily. "But even You have to admit my life basically sucks these days."

She was twenty-two, unmarried, unemployed and no more than a week or two from delivering a baby. She was virtually back on a doorstep she'd vowed she wouldn't cross again until she'd made something of herself and done it totally on her own without the Adams power and influence behind her. If she'd taken one thing away from Texas with her, it had been the fierce Adams pride, the determination to buck everyone and chart her own path.

She supposed, in a manner of speaking, that she had. She had made a royal mess of things. No other Adams that she knew of had gone so far astray. She'd skated through college with grades no higher than they had to be. She'd lied about who she was and run away more times and from more places than she could count. Rather than upholding the noble Adams tradition, she'd thumbed her nose at it. Oh, yes, she'd made something of herself, all right, but she wasn't especially proud of it, and this was hardly the triumphant homecoming she'd once envisioned.

The only thing she had going for her was the absolute certainty that the two people inside would welcome her back with open arms and without making judgments. Luke and Jessie Adams accepted people for who they were, flaws included. That went double for their only child, the daughter they adored. They would be relieved that she'd finally realized that her heart and her identity were all wrapped up with the tight-knit family who'd been patiently waiting for her all this time.

As she huddled in the rapidly cooling car, she recalled the oft-told story of the joy with which she'd been welcomed into the world twenty-three years ago tomorrow. She had been born in the middle of a Texas blizzard with no one around to assist her mother except Luke Adams, her uncle at the time and the man who became her father. Luke had been blind drunk that night, but he'd sobered in a hurry when faced with the immediacy of those shattering labor pains. He had risen to the occasion like a true Adams hero.

From an early age Angela understood that they both considered her to be their Christmas blessing, a miracle on a cold and bitter night. With her natural father dead, her birth had brought Luke and Jessie together, helped them to overcome the anguish and guilt they'd felt at having fallen in love even before her father's fatal accident. Just as her name implied, she was their angel. Living up to such a lofty label had been daunting.

Admittedly, though, their expectations for her probably hadn't been half as exalted as she'd imagined them to be. She hadn't done a lot of listening before breaking the ties with home. At the first opportunity, she had fled Texas, first to attend college, then to roam the country in search of herself. It was time, she had thought, to do something totally outrageous, to discover what she was truly made of. Being angelic was a bore. She wanted to be wicked or, if not actually wicked, at least human.

Unfortunately, even after four years at Stanford and a year on her own the answers still eluded her. Over the past few months she'd had plenty of empty nights to examine her past. She was human, all right. The very human mistakes were mounting up.

She'd made the worst miscalculation of all in Montana with a rancher named Clint Brady, a low-down scoundrel if ever there was one, she thought bitterly. Her mound of a belly was testament to that. She wasn't looking forward to the hurt and worry that her parents would try their best to hide when they saw her and realized just how much trouble she'd managed to get herself into. She hated the thought of the heartbreak she would read in their eyes.

She was less worried about the reaction of her incredible grandfather, Harlan Adams. When it came to family, he was thoroughly predictable. He would probably set off fireworks to celebrate the birth of his first great-grandbaby. If he had questions about the baby's conception, he'd keep them to himself.

For the time being, anyway, she amended. As meddlesome as he was capable of being, he wouldn't be silent for long. By year's end he'd probably have a lynch mob searching for the baby's father, assuming he could get Angela to name him, which she had no intention of doing. Not even Clint Brady deserved to face the rancor of the Adams men, once they'd been riled up.

In addition to Luke and her grandfather, there were Cody and Jordan. They might be wildly different in some ways, but they all shared the Adams gene for pure cussedness and family loyalty. Clint wouldn't have a prayer against the four of them. He'd be hogtied and married to her before he could blink. She would have no more say in the matter than he did.

To her chagrin, just the thought of Clint and her wild and reckless behavior in Montana made her blood run hot. Until she'd met him, she'd had no idea that passion could be so overwhelming, so completely and irresistibly awe inspiring.

Nor had she known how quickly passion could turn to hatred and shame.

She was glad now that she'd lied to him, that she'd faked a whole identity so that she could pretend for just a little while that she wasn't Luke and Jessie Adams's little angel. It had been liberating to pretend to be Hattie Jones, a woman with no exalted family history to live up to, a woman who could be as outrageous as she liked without regrets.

The decision to lie had been impulsive, made in a darkened country-western bar where she'd stopped to ask about a waitressing job that had been posted in the window. Clint had had the kind of lazy smile and sexy eyes that made a shy, astonishingly innocent college graduate imagine that all sorts of forbidden dreams were hers for the taking.

The job had been forgotten as she'd succumbed to newly discovered sensuality she hadn't even been tempted to test with the boys she'd met at Stanford. By the end of the night they were lovers. By the end of the week, she had moved in with him. She supposed that there was yet more irony that after all her running, she'd wound up with a rancher, after all.

More than once in the blissful days that followed she had regretted the casual lie she'd told when they met. More than once she had vowed to tell him the truth about who she was and where she came from, but Clint had been the kind of man who lived in the here and now. He didn't talk about his own past. He never asked about hers.

As weeks turned into months, it seemed easier to live with the lie. She liked being devil-may-care Hattie Jones, who flirted outrageously and never gave a thought to tomorrow. She liked the way Clint murmured her name in the middle of the night, as if he'd never before heard a word so beautiful.

In Clint's arms she was ecstatically happy. His ranch was a fraction of the size of her father's or her grandfather's, the days were long and exhausting, but none of that mattered, not at night when they made magic together. She found peace on that tiny Montana spread and something she had thought was love.

Then she'd discovered she was pregnant, and all of the lies and secrets between them—most of them admittedly her doing—had threatened to come unraveled.

When Clint had reacted in stunned silence to the news they were expecting a baby, that famous Adams pride had kicked in with a vengeance. She'd shouted a lot of awful, ugly things and he'd responded in kind. Even now the memory of it made her shudder.

If he'd been that furious over the baby, she couldn't imagine what his rage would be like once he discovered that she'd lied to him from the start. In her entire life, no one had ever made her feel so low. Nor had she ever before wanted to hurt a person so deeply that he would never recover from it. Words were their weapons and they had used them well.

Angela hadn't waited for tempers to cool. She'd loaded up her car and hit the road before dawn, determined to put Clint Brady and Montana far behind her.

That had been nearly seven months ago. She'd been in a lot of cities since. Few of them had even

registered. She had no more than vague memories of
cheap hotels and back-road diners.

She wasn't exactly sure when she'd realized that
Clint was following her. It had been almost a sixth
sense at first, a nervous knotting in the pit of her
stomach, a prickly sensation scampering down her
spine. She was too hurt, too sure that she'd been
wrong to get involved with him, too ashamed of her
age-old predicament to let him catch her. What was
the point of one more argument, anyway? It was best
to put him in the past, along with all the other mistakes she'd made. A fresh start beckoned from
around every curve in the road.

To her surprise, Clint hadn't given up easily. He'd
nearly caught up with her in Wyoming, cutting short
the part-time waitressing job she'd taken to get gas
money to move on. Warned about the man who'd
been in earlier asking questions about her, she'd
slipped out the diner's back door just as Clint came
through the front.

The narrow escape had made her jittery for days.
She hadn't felt secure until she'd managed to trade
her beloved blue convertible in for cash and a sensible beige sedan so old she hadn't even been born
the year it was made. No car that old should have
been expected to survive the kind of journey she'd
taken it on.

She had moved quickly on to Colorado, then dou-
bled back north to Cheyenne, looped up to South
Dakota, then headed west to Seattle, enchanted by
the idea of living by the water.

In Seattle she'd found a one-room apartment in an
area called Pill Hill for all the hospitals clustered

together. For the first time she had searched until she landed a halfway decent job as a receptionist. She'd found a kindly obstetrician to make sure she was doing all the right things for the baby she'd already learned to cherish. She'd vowed that the baby would never have to pay for the mistakes she'd made. Oddly enough, though being Angela Adams had daunted her, being a single mom did not.

In Seattle she'd even made a few friends, older, married women who invited her over often for home-cooked meals and the kind of nurturing concern she'd missed since leaving home. She took endless walks along Elliott Bay, bought fresh produce and fish at Pike's Place Market, sipped decaf cappuccino in every Starbucks she passed.

Clint seemed to have lost her trail or else he'd just given up and gone home, satisfied that he'd made a noble attempt to find her. No doubt that enabled him to sleep well enough. By then, he was probably sharing his bed with some other woman. At any rate, she'd felt it was safe to linger in Seattle. Contentment seemed almost within her grasp. She couldn't bring herself to admit that she was disappointed that he had given up.

Maybe, if it hadn't been for the Seattle weather, she could have made it work. But as summer gave way to fall and then to a premature winter, all that rain and gloom had finally gotten to her. She began to miss clear blue skies and the kind of heat that baked the earth.

When she packed up and moved on, she told herself her goal was merely sunshine. The undeniable truth was, she was heading straight for Texas, toward home.

For better or worse, she was going back to become Angela Adams again. The spirited Hattie Jones had died in Montana. Like it or not, Angela Adams was a Texan through and through. Her baby would be, too. The heritage she had abandoned for herself, she had no right to dismiss for the baby. It should be up to her child to decide someday if being an Adams was too much of a burden.

Not that she ever sat down and listed all the pros and cons for going home. The choice was instinctive. She'd hardly even needed a map to guide her south along the Pacific Coast and then east. If she'd stopped to reason it out, she probably would have found a hundred excuses for staying as far away from Texas as she could.

She'd developed a bad case of jitters near the end and wound up in Dallas, bypassing the turn to the south that would have taken her home much sooner. For days she'd lingered, wandering around the stores that had been decorated for the holidays, pretending that maybe this would be the final destination. It was close enough to home for an occasional visit, but far enough away to maintain her independence.

This afternoon, though, she had gotten into her car and impulsively started driving, taking familiar turns onto back roads and straight highways that were unmistakably leading her back to Los Pinos. Her static-filled radio had crackled with constant threats of an impending blizzard, but she hadn't once been tempted to turn back or to stop. Not even the first flurries of snow or the blinding curtain of white that had followed daunted her. Home beckoned by then with an inevitability she couldn't resist.

It was ironic, of course, that it had been on a night very much like this that her mother had gone into labor practically on Luke Adams's doorstep, had delivered Angela in his bed, with his help.

That had worked out well enough, she reminded herself as she tried to work up the courage to leave the safety and comfort of the car for the bitter cold walk home. Their marriage was as solid and secure as a bank vault.

Maybe that was why Angela had run from Clint Brady, had kept on running even when she knew he was chasing after her, even when she realized that it was possible that he wanted her back. She had seen what it could be like for two people who were head over heels in love, who faced problems squarely and grew strong because of them. She wanted nothing less for her child. If she couldn't offer the baby that, then she could at least make sure there was a wide circle of family around to shower her son or daughter with love.

As if in agreement, her baby kicked ferociously. Boy or girl, she thought defiantly, the kid was definitely destined to be a place kicker in the NFL. She rubbed her stomach and murmured soothing words, then drew in a deep breath.

Exiting the car to face an icy blast of air, she shivered and drew her coat more snugly around her.

"Okay, little one," she whispered as excitement stirred deep inside her, overcoming dread or at least tempering it. "This is it. Let's go home."

Chapter Two

Clint Brady had always possessed the kind of charm that could get him out of jams and, just as easily, into trouble. It was a blessing and a curse. Recently, he'd spent a lot of time regretting that he'd wasted a single ounce of it on Miss Hattie Jones. She'd been nothing but trouble.

Drawn to her blue eyes and dark auburn hair, enchanted by her from-the-gut laughter, seduced by a body that curved and dipped like a Rocky Mountain road, he'd tossed aside common sense and set out to get her into his bed. There'd been half a dozen years age difference between them, but he'd dismissed that as if it had been no more than a minute.

Even when half of what she'd said hadn't added up any better than his books at the end of the month, he'd dismissed reason and run with his hormones.

He should have been old enough and smart enough to know better, which just proved how wrong things could go when a man started thinking with something other than his brain.

Even so, for the better part of a year, he hadn't regretted his decision. That choice had set them off on one heckuva steamy ride. Hattie had been like no woman he had ever known before—sweetly vulnerable one minute, a wickedly sensuous vixen the next. His life had been filled with an incomparable mix of unexpected laughter and impromptu sex. They hadn't been able to get enough of each other. They'd learned to strip faster than a cook could shuck an ear of corn.

Yet for all of Hattie's spontaneity in the bedroom, she'd had a head filled with commonsense advice and straight thinking. He'd admired that almost as much as he had her generosity in bed.

For a man who'd never known the meaning of permanence, not when it came to relationships, anyway, he had actually started to think about forever. The prospect had scared him worse than the first time he'd crossed paths with a bear and twice as badly as dancing away from a rattler.

Right square in the middle of his panic, she'd dropped the news that she was pregnant. She'd stared at him over a candlelit dinner and said the words straight out, as blunt as a dare and twice as challenging. He figured there wasn't a man on God's earth that would blame him for being temporarily stunned into silence.

Women, on the contrary, obviously expected a

more immediate and more joyous response. Before he'd been able to gather his wits, before they could have anything resembling a rational discussion of their options, Hattie had come completely unglued. She'd hurled a bunch of accusations in his direction, then added that she was no more interested in commitment than he was. She'd verbally blasted the hard life she'd had living with him and had followed that almost immediately with the intentionally cruel announcement that she'd be giving the baby up for adoption and that he'd be the last man on earth she'd allow to claim any child of hers.

Shaken by her venom, Clint had shouted good riddance as she'd flown out the door. The echo of car doors slamming had been as sweet a sound as he had ever heard.

Naturally as soon as she was gone, though, he'd calmed down and changed his mind. He hadn't been able to stop thinking about a little blue-eyed, red-haired girl or boy who'd grow up to take over the small ranch he owned in Montana. He'd finally have the family he'd always secretly longed for, but had convinced himself was out of reach as long as he was living such a hand-to-mouth existence. With a few hours of peace and quiet to soothe his frayed temper, the sound of wedding bells hadn't seemed nearly so discordant.

Unfortunately, Hattie was long gone by the time he came to his senses. He had been fool enough to figure that she would come back when she calmed down, that they would work it out. In all the months they'd been together, he'd somehow missed the fact that Hattie had a temper to match that red hair of hers.

By dawn he'd begun to realize that he'd misjudged the depth of her fury. By noontime, he was calling himself every kind of fool for letting her get away. By four he was on the road, chasing down a trail that was already growing cold. No one in town had seen her go. She hadn't even stopped for gas.

He spent two blasted weeks he couldn't spare playing cat and mouse with a woman who clearly didn't want to be caught. When she ducked out the back door of a diner in Wyoming just as he came in the front, he blistered the air with a string of curses that could have been heard clear back in Montana. It was pure luck he'd been able to get a grip on himself before the sheriff had shown up to check out the lunatic on the premises.

He told himself he'd had it, that she didn't matter, that the world would keep on turning if he never set eyes on her again. He no longer allowed himself to picture his baby at all. It hurt too much to think that he'd never even know if he had a son or daughter.

Back home with spring just around the corner, he worked the ranch every day until his back ached and sweat poured off his brow. He collapsed into bed each night, exhausted, but with his mind still alive with images of Hattie and his body aching for her touch.

Then, despite his best efforts to keep them at bay, the images of their baby flooded in, the child he would never know if he left things as they were. He'd grown up fatherless, the youngest in a long line of kids and apparently the straw that broke his father's back. His dad had left the day he was born. His own brothers and sisters had resented him from the beginning, had blamed him for their dad's leaving. Only his mother had cared that he was alive. She was the only one with whom he'd kept in touch. It was easier on all of them if he kept his distance.

No one on earth knew better than he what it was like to wonder, what it was like to yearn for a father's smile, for a sense of identity that only a father could give. No kid of his should have to go through that. No kid of his would ever have a minute's worry that he was unlovable, that it was his fault that his dad wasn't around.

And so he'd started the search all over again, picking up a clue here, another there, using a private detective when he could afford one, his own instincts when he couldn't. At least once a month he was on the road, following a lead, showing a snapshot of a smiling Hattie, sitting on a low-hanging branch of a tree, skirt hitched up to her thighs. That picture had grown faded and blurred from handling, but her smile was still enough to make his heart ache.

He was way past desperation now. By his calculations the baby was due any minute and there were times it seemed he was no closer to finding Hattie than he had been seven months ago. The trail of slim leads from the last detective had ended in Dallas where she'd been spotted at a cafe. It was a huge city with lots of nooks and crannies a woman could hide in, if she was of a mind to, which Hattie certainly was.

Depressed by the needle-in-a-haystack enormity of the task facing him, Clint took refuge in a diner, the sort of cheap, inconspicuous place he'd discovered Hattie was drawn to. The too-bright lights glared off yellowing Formica and scarred chrome that had been polished until it managed a faint sparkle.

The tired colored lights on a tiny artificial Christmas tree winked on and off erratically, reminding him that it was a season of joy and wonder. The place smelled of stale grease and fresh coffee. The jukebox mourned lost love. If crying had been in his nature, Clint would have wept.

"Hey, sugar, you look like a man who needs a drink worse than he needs the kind of grub you'll get in this place."

Clint looked up from the laminated menu and found himself staring into sparkling brown eyes. Unruly blond hair had been partially tamed into a luxuriant ponytail. Lush, upturned lips, which would have made his pulse race a year ago, did little more than draw a returning smile now. The tag on her pocket said her name was Betsy.

"Betsy, are the burgers juicy and big?" he asked.

"Big enough to shut down half a dozen arteries before you can say bypass surgery," she responded.

"Is the coffee hot and strong?"

"Sugar, it'll make the hair on your chest curl," she said, her gaze pinned on that particular part of his anatomy as if she could see straight through his shirt.

Clint nodded. "Then I'm in the right place, after all. Two burgers and keep the coffee coming." He glanced around, assured himself that he was the only customer, then added, "And I'll double your tip if you pull the plug on that jukebox."

"What's the matter?" she inquired with a touch of feigned indignation. "You don't like country?"

"Under the right circumstances, I love country music."

Her expression radiated understanding. "It's just that you're so low-down, you don't want to be reminded of it."

"Exactly."

She silenced the jukebox and left him alone after that, except to bring his food and refill his coffee cup half a dozen times. The last time, as the clock ticked on toward midnight, she lingered.

"Sure you don't want to talk about it? I've got nothing to do tonight but listen."

Clint couldn't see the point in talking, but he couldn't much see the point to keeping silent, either. He poured out the whole sad tale, while Betsy clucked and sympathized.

"So, let's see this woman who has you all tied up in knots," she said eventually. "You have a picture of her?"

He dragged out the snapshot and pushed it across the counter. Expecting no more than a glib comment about Hattie's beauty, he wasn't prepared for the quick, indrawn breath or the suddenly cautious expression.

"What did you say her name was again?"

"Hattie," he told her. "Hattie Jones."

"No way," Betsy said, then clamped her lips together as if she'd already said too much.

"You recognize her, don't you?" Clint demanded, his hopes soaring for the first time in months. "Has she been in here? Did she work here?"

"Heck, no," she said as if the idea were totally preposterous.

The reaction startled him. He'd always thought Hattie was a high-class woman, but she surely wasn't above an honest day's hard work in a diner.

"What, then? How do you know her? What name's she going by now?" he asked. It would be no surprise to discover she'd taken an assumed name. Nothing about Hattie surprised him anymore, including the fact that she was quicksilver fast at slipping away from him.

"Her own, I imagine."

"And that would be?"

Betsy stared hard, straight into his eyes. "What'd you say you wanted with her? Give me the bottom line."

"I told you before, we have some unfinished business. That baby of ours needs a daddy and I intend to be one."

"You aiming to marry her?" Betsy prodded.

"That's one possibility," he conceded, though he wondered if that particular answer wasn't out of the question. Hattie had made her opinion of him plain as day by running from him time and again.

"And the others?" Betsy asked.

"We'll work something out about the baby." Clint offered up a full-wattage smile, the kind he'd been told was irresistible to women. "Come on, Betsy. I saw that book you were reading. You're a sucker for a happy ending, aren't you? Help me out here."

Betsy appeared to weigh his response before saying, "I hope to hell I'm not making a mistake."

"You're not," Clint reassured her, then held his breath and waited. He thought he'd won Betsy's trust, but he was equally certain that something about Hattie was making her hesitate. Did she have a new boyfriend the size of a Dallas Cowboys linebacker? Or had she simply sworn Betsy to secrecy? Whatever the explanation, he saw the wariness in Betsy's eyes give way to determination.

"Her name's Angie," she said evenly. "Angela Adams."

She said it without the slightest hint of uncertainty that would come with recent acquaintance. In fact, she said it with the confidence of someone who'd known her long and well. Better than he had, maybe.

"Angie Adams," he repeated, testing the name on his tongue. "You're sure?"

"Sugar, she and I went all through school together, first grade right on through graduation. Of course, that's when I quit, but last I heard Angie was going off to some fancy college in California." Her brow creased. "Stanford, maybe. That was five, no, almost six years back. She'd be out by now."

If Hattie had been to Stanford, then Clint had a degree in nuclear physics. She'd been looking for a job in a low-class bar the night they'd met. He doubted Stanford gave out degrees in waitressing.

"It can't be the same person," he insisted.

"Then Angie has a twin," she replied just as adamantly.

"You haven't seen her recently, have you?"

"Not since graduation. Seemed like she couldn't put enough distance between herself and home."

"What about her family? Are they here in Dallas?"

"Heck, no. They're over in Los Pinos. They practically own the whole town and most of the land surrounding it. Her granddaddy was the biggest rancher in the state till he turned the family spread over to her Uncle Cody. Her daddy's the second biggest. Her Uncle Jordan owns an oil company."

Hattie? Clint thought incredulously. Hattie, who'd been having a tough time scraping together food money when he'd met her?

Suddenly, though, dozens of tiny evasions began to make sense. Her familiarity with ranching, despite her claim that she'd never set foot on one, took on new significance. She'd pitched in with chores as if she'd done them before, but she'd sworn she was just a quick study. He'd been too glad of the willing help to cross-examine her. Now it seemed as if his tendency to live and let live had been a big mistake. He should have started asking questions the day she appeared in that bar.

If she'd lied about her name and her background, what else had she lied about? Who the hell was Hattie Jones, after all? Had she even been pregnant when she'd left or had that been just another in the series of lies? Maybe she'd just been testing the depth of his affections and he'd failed the test, so she'd moved on to greener pastures.

Then again, she was awful close to home. If she'd been avoiding it for all these years as Betsy claimed, what would bring her back if not the impending birth of a baby? An heir to all this Adams wealth that Betsy had been describing? There was only one way he could think of to get answers.

"Can you tell me exactly how to get to her parents' place?"

"Better yet, I'll show you," Betsy offered. "I've got a whole week off and I was planning on heading over to Los Pinos for Christmas as soon as my shift ends at one. My car's been conking out on me a lot lately, though. If I can hitch a ride with you, I'll take you straight to their front door."

She winked at him. "And just in case things don't work out, I'll point the way to my folks' place. It's not as fancy as theirs, but you'll be welcome."

Clint didn't want to give her any false expectations. Betsy was a nice woman, but she was no Hattie. Who knew, though? Once he'd decided whether or not to strangle the woman who'd walked out on him, a straight shooter like Betsy might start looking pretty good.

"Let's see how this turns out," he said. "If this Angie Adams is the right woman, I'll owe you."

"Sugar, it's not your wallet I'm interested in." Her expression turned resigned. "But a few bucks is all you're likely to part with, isn't it? You really do have it bad, don't you?"

He wasn't about to admit just how bad. He settled

for offering a warning. "Betsy, you don't want anything to do with a man like me. Just ask your old friend Angie. I'm sure she'd be eager enough to tell you all my flaws."

"Sugar, working in a place like this, I learned a long time back to be a good judge of character. You look just fine to me. Besides, Angie never did know when she had it good. Wait till you see that spread she grew up on. If she could turn her back on that, she doesn't have the sense the good Lord gave a duck. You'd be better off with a woman who appreciates you."

There was a time, Clint thought, when no one had appreciated him better than Hattie had. It was his fault that that had changed. In one lightning-quick moment of frozen panic, he'd destroyed all they'd had together. He was willing to accept responsibility for that much, anyway.

Or was he entirely to blame? Maybe Hattie was just the kind of woman who had to keep on moving on, who'd instigate a fight so she could go. Maybe she was just a natural-born liar. Could be he wasn't the first man she'd run out on or the first one she'd lied to.

After months of feeling angry and lonely by turns, he was about to find the woman who'd tied him in knots. He'd settle things with her once and for all. For the first time they would put all their cards on the table and decide where they stood. He'd find out if she was even capable of telling the truth.

He hoped so. He really did, because no conniving,

lying woman would get the chance to raise a child of his. If he didn't like what he discovered, their baby would be going back to Montana with him. She could bet the whole fancy Adams ranch on that.

Chapter Three

Coming home had been a hundred times worse than Angela had anticipated and a thousand times better.

She had seen first shock, then joy register on her parents' faces as they'd realized who was ringing their bell and waking them out of a dead sleep. If she'd kept her old key, she could have crept in unnoticed and greeted them over breakfast in the morning, when she had her own emotions under better control. As it was, she'd dragged them out of bed, stunned them first with her return, then dismayed them with a refusal to answer a single question about the baby she was so obviously carrying. The tearful reunion had taken on a confrontational tone very quickly.

"Dammit, I want to know who's responsible for

the condition you're in," her father had bellowed loudly enough to raise the rafters.

"I am," she had replied quietly.

He glared at her. "Unless things have changed a helluva lot more than I realized, you didn't get pregnant on your own. Where's the father of this baby? Are you married?"

Angela regarded him in stoic silence.

"Luke, that's enough," her mother had said eventually, when it was clear they were at a standoff.

As always, her touch on his cheek was more effective at quieting him than her words. Angela had always envied them that, the ability to communicate with a touch, a glance.

"Can't you see she's worn-out and shivering?" her mother had chided. "It must be below freezing outside. Come into the kitchen right this second and let me make you some hot chocolate."

"I'd rather have tea," Angela said, casting a wary look at her father's grim expression as he followed them into the kitchen. "Herbal, if you have it."

"Of course I have it," her mother said as she filled the teakettle with water and put it on the stove. "Consuela insists we keep wild blackberry tea in the house just for you. It was always your favorite."

"How is she?" Angela asked, smiling, relieved by the chance to change the topic. "I thought for sure she'd be retired by now. She must be what? Eighty-something?"

"Eighty-two and as spry as ever. She wears me out and she flatly refuses to retire," her mother said. "She says she won't have someone else in her kitchen. She'll be over the moon in the morning when she finds out you're home. She's been baking your favorite cookies for the past week. She swears something told her you'd be back this year. Nothing we said could dissuade her."

Guilt rippled through Angela. Consuela had been far more than a housekeeper. She had been the grandmother Angela had never had. She'd taken a terrible chance not staying in touch with her. At Consuela's age anything could have happened and Angela would never have known.

"I'm sorry I haven't been in touch, especially this past year. I'm sorry I didn't let you know I was coming."

"Nonsense. It doesn't matter. You're here now." Her mother glanced at her father. "Isn't that right, Lucas?"

His stony expression softened just a fraction. "Of course we're glad you're home, angel. We've missed you."

Tears welled up in her eyes at the hurt she heard in his voice. "I'm sorry," she said, her own voice choked. "I'm sorry for everything."

"Oh, baby, you don't have anything in the world to apologize for. You may not believe it, but we both understood exactly why you felt you had to go. Didn't we, Luke?"

"That's true enough. We didn't like it, but nobody knows better than we do what it takes to be an Adams in these parts," he said, his expression wry. "I fought it in my way. Your uncles fought it in theirs. You just ran a little farther than the rest of us."

"The bottom line is we love you," her mother said. "And we are both very glad you're home again where you belong." She hesitated. "You are here to stay, aren't you?"

Angela wished she could claim that she was just passing through, that she had a home and a life of her own to get back to once the holidays were over, but she couldn't. "If you'll have me," she said, no longer able to control the tears that had been threatening ever since she'd crossed the threshold.

Her father reached over and brushed the dampness from her cheeks. "There was never any doubt about that. Never."

Angela could feel their love warming her, chasing away all the fears and loneliness of the past few months. Once she had felt smothered by that love, choked by the overly protective nature of her whole extended family, from Grandpa Harlan and her strong-willed uncles right on down to the two people in this room. Not anymore. She realized now just how desperately she had been longing for this kind of unconditional acceptance. For the past couple of months her nesting instinct had been kicking in with a vengeance.

After her father's initial outburst, her parents had held their questions about the baby she was expecting. They had filled her with hot tea and thick ham sandwiches and a half-dozen Christmas cookies before sending her off to bed in the room that hadn't changed a bit since she'd left it behind. Consuela had kept it swept and dusted, but the old concert posters were still on the walls, and her menagerie of stuffed animals still tumbled across the bed.

She'd heard her parents' whispers as they'd gone off to their own room and known that the reprieve from questions wouldn't last forever. It wasn't in her father's nature to let one of his own be hurt without taking action to see that it never happened again. Even as he'd fallen silent after her mother's soft reproach, Angela had noticed the stubborn, determined jut of his chin. Her mother's intervention had only managed to delay the inevitable until this morning.

As Angela stood at the foot of the steps and tried to work up the courage to enter the dining room for breakfast, she braced herself for the new barrage of questions that he'd been forced to hold back the night before. She vowed to tell them as little as she could get away with. She ought to be very good at evasions by now. She'd been practicing long enough. She'd perfected the technique in Rocky Ridge, Montana.

She drew in a deep breath and stepped into the dining room. Her mother and father looked up when they heard her, and smiles spread across their faces.

Before she could even summon up a returning smile, she was enveloped in the arms of a plump Mexican woman whose once-black hair had gone almost completely white. There were new lines carved into her olive complexion, but her dark brown eyes sparkled as merrily as ever.

"Ah, *niña,* you are home," Consuela murmured, stroking Angela's hair back from her face as she had when she was a child. A rapid stream of Spanish that was part welcome, part chastisement followed until

Angela laughed and pressed a finger against the housekeeper's lips.

"Despacio, por favor," she pleaded. "Slowly, Consuela. I've forgotten every bit of Spanish you taught me."

"Then you must practice," Consuela said briskly. "It will be good for the baby, too. He will grow up bilingual."

"He?" Angela said, grinning at the assumption.

"Of course. I know these things." Consuela scowled at Luke, who hadn't bothered to hide his skepticism. "You laugh? Did I not predict the sex of every child ever born in this family, starting with you and your brothers?"

"That was easy. No girl had been born in the Adams clan for a hundred years," Luke teased.

"And what of Cody's daughter? Or your stepsister?" Consuela countered indignantly. "They were not so easy to predict, yes?"

"Okay, okay, I surrender," he said. "You know these things."

"Indeed," Consuela said. "Now, *niña,* what can I fix for you? Waffles, eggs, a Spanish omelet, perhaps?"

"The omelet," Angela said eagerly, her hands on her swollen belly. She grinned. "And the waffle. For the baby."

"Of course," Consuela said, bustling off to the kitchen to work her magic.

Angela sat down opposite her mother, aware of the worried glances she kept casting at her husband. Apparently she was anticipating the flood of questions, just as Angela was. Only Consuela seemed willing to accept her condition as a simple fact of life and not cause for an inquisition.

"Where have you been for the past year and a half?" her father asked oh, so casually, in what for him was a dramatic show of diplomacy. "Aside from an occasional call to say you were OK, we haven't heard so much as a word from you since you graduated from college. You never gave us so much as a post office box, so we could contact you."

"I was traveling most of that time," she said. It was the truth as far as it went.

"Obviously you stayed in one place a little too long," her father retorted.

"Luke!" her mother said sharply.

He scowled. "Dammit, we have a right to know the truth."

"Only if Angela wants to tell us," her mother countered. "She's a grown woman."

The unfamiliar dissension between the two of them set her nerves on edge. Worse, she hated being the cause of it. "I can't tell you," she said with regret.

"What do you mean you can't?" Luke demanded, bellowing again. "Don't you even know who the father of the baby is?"

Angela stared at him in shock. "Of course, I know."

"Then is it asking too much to expect you to tell us?"

"It is if you're going to go ballistic and start making trouble,'' she shot back. "I'm here. The father's not. That should pretty much settle things.''

"Nothing's settled, as far as I can tell. I'd say that trouble you're afraid I'll stir up is already here. I'm just trying to figure out how to clean up after it.''

Angela trembled at the sound of barely contained rage in his voice. It was exactly what she'd anticipated, what she'd feared she would be stirring up by coming home.

"Maybe I should go,'' she said softly.

"Absolutely not,'' her mother snapped, adding in a rare display of temper, "Luke, that's enough. Let's everybody calm down.''

Her father looked as if he were ready to explode. "Fine. You get the truth out of her, then,'' he said, throwing his napkin onto the table and stalking out.

"Don't mind him,'' her mother apologized. "He's just worried about you. We both are.''

"There's no need to worry. I'm fine.''

"Sweetie, if you were fine, you wouldn't have been on our doorstep, half-frozen in the middle of the night. I know you. You came home because you felt you didn't have anyplace else to go. You have too much pride to have come home otherwise.''

The all-too-accurate assessment brought the sting of tears to her eyes. "Maybe I just missed you.''

"Maybe you did, but that alone wouldn't have been enough to get you back here, not after you made such an issue of staying away,'' her mother said dryly. "Now you can tell *me* what's going on, or you can tell your father, or you can keep it all bottled up inside.''

Angela grinned ruefully. "Those are my only choices?"

"Unless you'd rather tell your grandfather," her mother retorted. "No doubt he'll be on his way over as soon as he hears you're back. He's expected tomorrow, anyway. I doubt I'll be able to keep him away. He's been just itching to put a private eye on your trail for the past year and a half. When he sees you're pregnant, there won't be a place on earth the father of that baby can hide."

Angela thought of Clint's efforts to track her down. He was a pure amateur compared to her grandfather, but he'd done a pretty good job of it just the same. "He hasn't exactly been hiding," she admitted. "He's been trying to find me for the last seven months."

Her mother's gaze narrowed. "But you've been determined to elude him? Why? Did he abuse you?" she demanded, her voice barely above a horrified whisper. "If that man harmed you in any way—"

"No," she said hurriedly. "He never laid a hand on me."

Obviously relieved, her mother's expression softened. Her gaze fell on Angela's stomach. "Oh, really?"

"I meant he never hurt me, not physically."

"Why did you run then?"

"He didn't want the baby," she said simply.

"Are you sure about that?"

She recalled in vivid detail the humiliation of sitting across that candlelit table from Clint, praying for a whoop of joy, even a smile, only to see that stunned, blank expression on his face. "He all but said it when I told him I was pregnant," she said.

"He all but said it," her mother repeated with a sad shake of her head. "Darling, if he was so anxious to be rid of you and the baby, why has he been chasing after you all this time?"

"I don't know."

"Don't you think you should try to find out? Don't you owe it to your child?"

"It's too late."

Her mother looked skeptical. "Tell me one thing, then. Did you love him?"

"I thought I did," Angela admitted softly, then forced her gaze to meet her mother's. "I was wrong. I just want to put it all behind me."

For a moment it looked as if her mother was going to argue, but then she nodded. "Well, you've certainly always known your own mind. If that's what you want, I'll do my best to keep Luke and your grandfather from stirring things up."

"It's what I want," Angela said firmly and without the slightest hesitation. Even as she spoke, though, a little voice deep inside shouted, "Liar." She'd heard that same accusation so often the past couple of years that she was able to ignore it one more time.

Four in the morning or not, if he'd had his way, Clint would have started pounding on Angela Adams's front door the minute he and Betsy got to Los Pinos, but she had persuaded him to wait until a more reasonable hour. She'd also promised to make a call to the ranch to see if the lady in question was, in fact, back home again. Small town or not, her parents hadn't heard any gossip about it yet, though there'd apparently been plenty of speculation over the years about Angela's disappearance.

A half hour ago, after he'd managed to catch a couple of hours sleep in a guest room at Betsy's parents' house, she had made the call. She'd quickly confirmed that Angela had arrived home unexpectedly just the night before. She hadn't dared to ask whether the prodigal daughter had arrived home more than eight months pregnant. Still, Clint couldn't help believing that he had found his "Hattie" at last.

Now he sat outside the gate to the ranch and tried to bring his temper under control. The sight of a decrepit beige sedan half-buried in a snowdrift a half-mile back only raised his hackles more. He'd lay odds that was the car she'd been driving.

He told himself repeatedly that there was no point in charging in and getting the whole family riled up. Betsy, who'd proved time and again to be one of the most sensible women he'd ever met, had convinced him that a man in his position didn't want the whole lot of Adams men squared off against him, especially on their home turf.

So he was cooling his heels and hopefully his anger. He'd spent the past couple of hours envisioning this confrontation, envisioning the way Hattie's eyes—no, *Angela's*, dammit—would widen with shock when she realized she'd been found out. He could hardly wait.

He put his pickup in gear and drove up the winding lane to the impressive house. It seemed to ramble forever, dwarfing his own ranch. Barns, stables, everything in sight was spit-and-polish perfect.

Hands jammed into his pockets, he forced himself to walk slowly up to the front door, fighting intimidation over his surroundings every step of the way.

His control wasn't quite strong enough to prevent him from leaning on the doorbell. He could hear the impatient chime echoing through the house.

"I'll get it, Mom," an all-too-familiar voice called out.

The sound of that sweet voice sent goose bumps chasing down Clint's spine. Up until now he supposed a part of him had been holding out hope that Betsy had been wrong, that Hattie was Hattie and that there'd been no monumental lie between them. Now there was no denying the truth. He'd been played for a fool.

After taking a look around at her daddy's spread, he could imagine just how pitiful his own ranch had seemed to her. No wonder she'd been so eager to put it behind her. What stumped him, though, was why it had taken her so long to hightail it back to her daddy's place.

When the door swung open, he got exactly the shocked reaction he'd been hoping for, but he doubted it was any greater than his own. Even though he'd known she should be in the final month of her pregnancy—if she hadn't lied to him about that, too—the reality of it stunned him.

With her formerly svelte body swollen with his baby, she was more beautiful than ever. Curves that had been intriguing enough before were lush and gloriously feminine. He couldn't seem to tear his gaze away from her stomach, where both of her hands had settled protectively. Instinctively he reached out to touch her, to feel this growing child she'd kept from him, but she jerked away and tried to slam the door in his face.

Fortunately she was a little too ungainly to be as quick as she needed to be to prevent him from slipping inside. He caught the toe of his boot in the crack of the door, then wedged it open until the rest of him could follow. He closed it securely, while she eyed him as warily as if he'd been a rattler already coiled for striking.

"Hello, Hattie. Looks like we have some things to talk about." To his everlasting irritation, his voice shook when he said it. She still had the power to make him weak-kneed and crazy with desire. He had wondered if she would, had prayed that she wouldn't. At best, he'd wanted to be consumed with hatred, at worst, ambivalent. He hadn't wanted to be practically struck dumb with longing. Add to that her ability to rile him, and it was a wonder he managed to get a word out at all.

"Not here," she whispered urgently. Her eyes pleaded with him. "Please, Clint. I'll meet you in town. Just give me an hour."

He shook his head. "I'd like to accommodate you, I really would, but you have this nasty habit of taking off on me. I don't think I'll chance it this time."

Just then a woman who looked like an older version of Hattie came down the hall and into the foyer.

She was tall and slender and radiant. She had the kind of self-possession and grace that attracted men and made women envious. Her glance shifted from Clint to her daughter, then back again. Apparently even she could sense the crackling tension in the air.

"Angie, is everything okay?"

Clint figured he'd let Hattie field that one. He fixed his gaze on her and watched the color bloom in her cheeks. Her shoulders sagged.

"Mother, this is Clint Brady," she said eventually. "The man I told you about."

Mrs. Adams's friendly expression vanished at that. "I think you should leave," she said, her voice stiff and formal. "You've caused enough pain."

"I swear to you that I don't want any trouble, ma'am, but I'm not leaving. Not until Hattie and I settle a few things," he said politely, but firmly.

His vehemence clearly took her aback. Apparently few people argued with her, confirming Betsy's description of a family used to being in control not only of its own destiny, but of most of the world around it.

She quickly regained her composure, then glanced at her daughter, her expression vaguely puzzled. "Hattie?"

Clint's lips curved as he observed Angela's unmistakable discomfort. "I guess you forgot to tell your mother some of the details."

"Clint, please," she begged.

Her mother took pity on her, even if Clint's patience was too far gone for him to.

"I think it's best if you go. You don't want to be

here when my husband gets back," Mrs. Adams insisted. "He has a quick temper and these circumstances call for some preparation."

Clint shrugged. "I figure your husband and I probably want the same thing about now..." He looked straight at Hattie. "Answers. I'm not leaving here without them."

Hattie sighed. Resignation spread across her face. "It's OK, Mother. I'll deal with this."

"Are you sure? I can call your father."

Hattie shook her head. "It's not necessary." She stared at him pointedly. "Clint's no threat to me."

Her mother backed down with obvious reluctance, leaving Hattie to lead the way into a living room that was almost the size of his whole ranch house. The money spent on the furnishings would have kept his place afloat for a year. The holiday decorations were as spectacular as any he'd ever seen in a department store, all gold and glitter and candlelight even at midmorning.

Clint and Angela stared at each other uneasily. He was trying to assess exactly where to begin. She looked as if she were girding for battle.

An older Mexican woman appeared almost at once, bearing a silver tray laden with coffee and freshly baked cinnamon rolls. There was also a cup of herbal tea, the wild blackberry kind he knew Hattie favored. Somehow he felt reassured by that small bit of evidence that she was still the same woman he'd fallen for in Montana.

"Thanks, Consuela," Hattie said distractedly.

"Thank you, ma'am," Clint said. "That coffee smells mighty good."

"You need anything else, you call, *niña*," she said to Hattie, then gave Clint an assessing once-over. Apparently whatever she saw pleased her, because she left the room with a satisfied smile on her lips. It appeared he had one person in his corner. Judging from Hattie's lack of welcome, he probably ought to count himself lucky that no one so far had aimed a shotgun his way.

"How do you do that?" Hattie said.

"What?"

"Mutter half a dozen words and charm the socks off a woman? First Mother backs down and Consuela practically swoons."

"It's a gift," he declared. He tried smiling at her. "Used to work on you, too, as I recall."

She didn't bat an eye. "That was then. This is now. How'd you find me?"

"Pure grit, *Hattie*."

"Drop the Hattie," she said irritably. "Obviously you've figured out by now that it isn't my real name."

"OK, Angela." He regarded her speculatively. "Something tells me, though, that around here they probably call you Angel."

The flood of color in her cheeks told him he'd hit the mark, but she ignored the observation.

"Maybe the more important question is why did you bother?" she asked.

Her expression was a mix of curiosity and an even deeper resignation. She actually looked vulnerable,

more vulnerable than he could ever recall Hattie
looking when she'd been dancing up a storm and
flirting with half the men in Montana.

"You're having my baby, unless you lied about
that, too, *Angela*."

"That didn't seem to matter to you when I told
you," she reminded him.

"That was then. This is now," he mimicked.
"I've been trying to catch up with you since the day
you left."

"I repeat, why?"

"Because no child of mine is going to grow up
without a father," he said simply, his gaze locked
with hers. A shudder seemed to wash over her, even
as a spark of pure defiance lit her eyes.

"It's not your decision," she retorted.

"Yes," he said softly. "It is. As of this minute,
I'm making it mine."

Chapter Four

Angela had her hands clenched so tightly in her lap that even her bitten-to-the-quick nails were cutting into her flesh. Clint Brady was the most arrogant, the most infuriating, the most insufferable man she had ever had the misfortune to cross paths with. He was going to make a pest of himself. She could feel it. His words flat-out guaranteed it. She had run out on him, which perversely made him want both her and the baby.

The truth was, though, he hadn't wanted either one of them when she'd been right under his nose and more than willing to stay. This display was just male pride kicking in, nothing more. She couldn't allow herself to get caught up in an emotional tug-of-war, not when Clint would eventually tire of it and leave.

She couldn't work herself up over his threats and taunts. If she did, she'd be an emotional wreck.

Reasoning that out made her feel marginally better, despite the grim glint in his eyes and the stubborn jut of his chin.

Unfortunately, she also had the awful, gut-sick feeling that once he got over his desire to throttle the man, her father was going to take to Clint the way bears took to honey. They spoke the same testosterone-laden language. Add to that their dedication to ranching and the two of them were like two peas in a pod.

It was ironic, really. She had run away from Texas to escape all that stubborn, macho nonsense. Until just this instant, with Clint scowling at her and insisting that he had rights here, she hadn't noticed that he was cut from the same cloth as all the Adams men she'd left behind. Just her luck.

"Go back to Montana," she pleaded one last time. "I'm home. I'm surrounded by my family. You don't need to worry about me or the baby."

"Maybe you should let me decide who needs worrying about," he said.

He said it in that sexy, laid-back tone she had once found incredibly seductive. Now it was merely patronizing and irritating. She wondered for a minute if his potent effect on her had finally worn off, but one long glance at him told her the emphatic answer to that. Her blood practically sizzled and she seemed to have no ability whatsoever to stop it.

Fixing her gaze on sun-streaked brown hair that needed trimming just to be respectable, blue eyes with a look of pure mischief in them and sensual lips capable of turning kissing into an art form, she knew she was far from over him. Just looking at him sent a jolt of desire slamming through her.

While she caught her breath, she realized that he was studying her just as intently.

"You look a little pale," he concluded. "Aren't you getting enough rest?"

"My color has nothing to do with exhaustion. I just keep getting an image of you with a bullet in your heart when my father finds you here," she said dryly.

"I had no idea you cared."

"Oh, for pity's sake, that wasn't a declaration of undying love. I'd feel the same about some poor, hapless animal walking past a hunter's shotgun."

He grinned. "Would you really? I guess that puts me in my place."

She glared at him. "Don't you dare mock me."

His expression sobered at once. "OK, I admit, we are getting a little far afield here. We have plans to make. Exactly when is the baby due?"

She saw little point in not telling him. It didn't take a genius in math to calculate the date with some degree of accuracy. Clint certainly ought to have the starting point pinned down well enough.

"Two weeks," she admitted grudgingly. "Though first babies are a little unpredictable, according to the doctor."

"Good, that gives us enough time, then."

She regarded him suspiciously. "Enough time for what?"

''To plan a wedding, of course.''

Angie's mouth dropped open. If he'd suggested brushing up on his medical skills so he could deliver the baby himself, she wouldn't have been any more stunned. ''A wedding? You and me? Have you completely lost your mind?''

He paused, his head tilted thoughtfully, then said, ''Nope. I don't think so. What kind of wedding do you want? Huge, I imagine, though it may be a little late in the day to try to pull that off. How about New Year's Eve? Something small and intimate. That ought to suit your sense of the romantic. Maybe right here in the living room, if your parents wouldn't object. The room could be lit with lots of candles.'' He glanced around deliberately. ''We're already halfway there on that score.''

Angela stared at him incredulously. He was serious. She recognized that stubborn glint in his eyes all too well. If she didn't stop him, he'd be ordering the rings and the flowers. Poinsettias in honor of the season, no doubt. The room would be a sea of red. She shuddered at the image.

Maybe if he'd said one single word about love, she would have catapulted herself straight into his arms. Instead, he'd set off warning bells. She saw the scheme for exactly what it was: a way to stake a legal claim on her baby. Well, she wouldn't be a party to it, and that was that.

If Clint Brady really wanted to be a father to this baby, then he was going to have to prove it, not with an impulsive wedding, but over time. Weeks, at the very least. Maybe months. As furious as she was, maybe even years.

"Forget it," she said softly. "No wedding. Obviously you've been sitting around the past few months with guilt weighing on your mind. That's OK. I always knew you were an honorable man. Now you've tracked me down and done the noble thing. You made me an offer of marriage, and I appreciate the gesture. I truly do. But it's not necessary. You can go on back to Montana and live your life exactly the way you want to with no commitments holding you back."

Before she could say another word, he had crossed the room and hauled her up off the sofa—no easy task, in her present condition. "Shut up," he murmured just before his mouth closed over hers.

His lips tasted like deep-roast coffee and felt like black velvet, sensuous and seductive, as they teased, then plundered. Clint had always known how to make a kiss memorable, and he was at his best this morning. Or maybe it was just that she'd been longing for another of his kisses for far too long. At any rate, this one was a doozy. Her resolve melted, right along with most of the muscles in her body. She felt like a limp noodle by the time he released her. A restless yearning had begun inside her, and she knew exactly where that was likely to lead unless she stopped this craziness. They'd be in front of a preacher by nightfall. Her father would encourage that notion right along.

"Oh, my," she murmured before she could stop

herself. So much for a display of resolve, she thought irritably.

"At least that hasn't changed," he said with obvious satisfaction.

"No," she conceded because there seemed to be little point in lying about it. His arms were just about the only thing between her and collapse and they both knew it.

She looked him square in the eye. "But it doesn't matter."

"Oh, it matters," he taunted. "It seems to me it's the only thing that does."

"Of course, you would say that. All that ever mattered to you was the sex. OK, I agree. We had spectacular, fireworks-caliber sex. Time stood still. The world rocked on its foundation. Adam and Eve would have envied us our total lack of inhibitions. So what?"

"So what?" he repeated softly. "You think that's unimportant?"

"In the overall scheme of things, yes," she said defiantly, even though that kiss had been potent enough to prove otherwise.

"Liar."

Angela shrugged. "I've been called worse, especially by you."

Clint sighed and for the first time he looked the slightest bit guilty. "Look, I know I didn't respond exactly the way you wanted me to when you told me about the baby."

Months of nursing hurt pride kept her temper up. "That's an understatement, if ever I've heard one."

"You took me by surprise, that's all. We hadn't talked about the future. We hadn't talked about the two of us, much less about a baby. You knew—"

"Did you or did you not say that a baby was the last thing you wanted?"

"I did, but—"

"Did you or did you not say that marriage was out of the question?"

"I did, but—"

She was on a roll now and had no intention of pausing for any of his fast-talking rationalizations. She'd been stewing over that night for months now. It felt good to have another chance to throw in a few more digs at his lousy behavior.

"Did you or did you not mean every low-down, spiteful, mean word you uttered that night?" she demanded.

"No."

That single word, spoken with soft vehemence, slowed her down. She regarded him skeptically. "Oh, really?"

Clint sighed. "OK, yes, at the time, I meant it."

"I rest my case."

"I didn't know we were having a damned trial here," he practically shouted.

Two worried faces promptly appeared in the doorway. "It's OK, Mom," Angela said hurriedly. "You and Consuela don't have to stand guard. Clint and I are just finishing a discussion we started several months ago."

Clint's cheeks turned a dull red as he apparently realized that every word they'd spoken had been overheard, that more than likely their kiss had been witnessed by two very interested parties.

Good, Angela thought. She was on her turf now. Let him suffer a little embarrassment and humiliation. Let him suffer the tortures of the damned, for that matter. In fact, she would have welcomed the arrival of her father just about now. She might even load his shotgun for him.

Even though Angela thought she'd made her dismissal of their observers plain, her mother stepped into the room, followed by the housekeeper. Obviously nobody intended to listen to a word she said this morning.

"Maybe we should all sit down and discuss this rationally," her mother suggested, a worried gaze locked on Clint.

"If you would like a New Year's Eve wedding, niña, I could have everything ready," Consuela offered eagerly. "It would be my joy."

Had everybody she knew turned deaf all of a sudden? Angela wondered irritably. "There is not going to be a wedding, not New Year's Eve, not ever," she said, her voice rising with each word. "Haven't I made myself clear? Clint will be leaving, going back to Montana, and that's final."

"I don't think so," Clint said quietly.

Consuela beamed at him, then chided Angela, "Maybe you should listen to him, niña. He seems very sincere."

"Oh, yes," Angela snapped. "He's about as sincere as a snake in the grass."

"Has she always been this stubborn?" Clint inquired as if she were no longer in the room.

Her mother smiled, clearly more than halfway ready to succumb to his charm, won over by his call for a wedding, even if it had come belatedly.

"Wait until you meet the rest of the family," she said. "She comes by it naturally. In fact, if you wouldn't mind a word of advice—"

That was it. That was the final straw. "Mother, I do not want you giving Clint Brady advice," Angela practically shouted, hoping that sheer volume would succeed, when nothing else had.

Her mother went on as if Angela had spoken in a whisper. "You might let her cool down a little, get used to the idea. I'm sure she'll be in a more receptive frame of mind in a few days. You could stay with us. You'll be able to meet the rest of the family. With the holidays coming, everyone will be here for a few days. And, of course, today is her birthday, so we'll be pulling together a last-minute party just for us, to celebrate. You can't miss that."

Clint Brady here, under the same roof? No way. Either her pragmatic mother was trying to make the best of an awful situation or she was getting back at Angela for running away from home in the first place.

"I do *not* want him in this house!" Angela insisted.

Despite the vehemence and shrill, escalating volume of her words, she had the distinct impression they were falling on deaf ears. Consuela leaped up and bustled off to ready the guest suite. Clint thanked her mother for the invitation and accepted without so much as a by-your-leave look in Angela's direction. She might as well have been invisible, she thought, thoroughly disgruntled by the turn of events.

Since no one seemed to give two hoots about what she thought, she hefted herself up off the sofa again and marched out of the room without a backward glance. If she hadn't been thoroughly exhausted from running, if she'd had anyplace else on earth to go, she would have fled the ranch and Texas and the overwhelming presence of Clint Brady.

Unfortunately, as she had all too recently discovered, there was apparently nowhere she could hide that he wouldn't find her. If there was going to be a grueling standoff, it might as well be where she could sleep in her own bed.

Luke Adams had the look of a man on a mission. Standing beside his pickup with his single piece of luggage, Clint observed Luke warily as he approached, hands jammed in the pockets of his jeans, a scowl etched in his rugged features and fire blazing in his eyes. He guessed it was going to be a tricky conversation.

They were about the same size and, despite the difference in their ages, probably equally fit. Ranching toughened a man at any age, and Luke had the look of a man who didn't leave the hard tasks to others. They had that in common, Clint thought optimistically. That and Angela, though he doubted her father would view the latter as a subject on which there could be much agreement.

"You're Brady?" Luke asked, regarding him distrustfully.

Clint offered his hand. Luke Adams ignored it. Clint guessed it was because he was scared to death if his hands came out of his pockets, one of them would land squarely in the middle of Clint's face. Clint couldn't blame him entirely for the reaction.

"I know this looks bad," he began.

"Bad?" Luke snapped. "Son, I figure you've got about thirty seconds to do some very fast talking to keep me from ripping you apart."

"I think I understand how furious you must be, but I swear to you that I am trying to get your daughter to marry me," Clint said. "I'm trying to do right by her and the baby."

"Shouldn't you have been thinking about that nine or ten months ago, before she wound up pregnant?"

"Nine or ten months ago the only thing on my mind was trying to keep my ranch afloat," Clint said honestly. "I figured I wouldn't have a whole lot to offer a woman, if it went under and I lost the land. Then Angela hit me with the news that she was pregnant and I panicked. I know I was wrong. Hell, I knew it even while we were still shouting at each other, but before things could calm down, she split. I've been chasing after her ever since, trying to put things right."

He realized that despite his anger over the discovery of all her lies, that was what he still wanted. He shook his head ruefully. "That woman moves faster than any oil slick and she's twice as slippery. Until now I've barely caught sight of her since the night she stormed out of my house.''

Luke pinned him with a penetrating look. ''Why'd you bother chasing her at all, if catching her was so much trouble?''

It was the same question Angela had asked, but Clint wasn't any more certain of the right answer now than he had been a few hours earlier.

''Because I wanted to do the right thing by her. Your daughter's a hell of a woman. And that baby, well, I may not have what you have here, but I am its daddy. I figure a child has a right to know the man responsible for bringing it into the world.''

To his surprise something in Luke Adams's expression softened. The harsh, down-turned lines around his mouth eased up just a fraction. It was not quite a smile, but Clint felt relieved nonetheless. The tension in the air lessened. The first step toward a grudging respect had been taken—or at least he hoped it had.

''Even though she swears she wants no part of you, are you planning on sticking around?'' Luke asked.

''Until I can talk her into marrying me,'' Clint vowed. He hadn't thought much beyond that. His first goal had simply been to make everything nice and legal. He'd figured that would be tricky enough without worrying about what the next step might be. He wanted an honest claim on that baby, if the matter ever wound up in court. He kept that particular motive to himself. After what Angela had done to him, he figured he was entitled to one devious act. A gambler would call it hedging his bets. Luke Adams probably wouldn't see it that way.

As it was, his declaration drew a full-fledged smile from his prospective father-in-law. "It won't be easy," Luke informed him. "She seems to have made up her mind to do this her way."

"I can be very persuasive when I have to be," Clint said with more confidence than was probably justified. Angela had shown some evidence of being able to resist his charms. That had been an unexpected turn of events. He'd thought that breezing in here and staking his claim was going to be easy. He wasn't exactly disturbed to find he'd been wrong. He loved a good challenge as well as the next man. It kept life interesting, especially if a woman like Angela was involved.

"We'll work it out," Clint promised.

Luke seemed to find his self-assurance amusing. "Good luck," he said. He started toward the house, then turned back, his expression sobering. "Just one more thing. I don't know the details of what went on between the two of you in the past, but you hurt that girl of mine again and this time you'll be answering to me. Do we understand each other?"

The warning was as plain as a six-shooter pointed at the gut. Clint's respect for Luke Adams tripled in that instant. Here was a man who fought for what was his, who fiercely protected those he cared about. He was exactly the kind of man—the kind of father—Clint intended to be.

"Perfectly," he said quietly. "We understand each other perfectly."

The only problem he foresaw was getting the message through to Angela.

"Mother, how could you invite that man to stay here?" Angela demanded as she paced her room in pure frustration. She was already feeling claustrophobic just thinking about his presence, and this house was five times the size of the one she and Clint had shared in Montana.

"It seemed the sensible thing to do, dear," her mother said blandly as she calmly folded the laundry Consuela had done earlier in the day. "You don't want him roaming all over the countryside talking about this situation with everyone he happens to meet, do you?"

"So this is some sort of bizarre protective custody to keep him from damaging my reputation?"

"Exactly."

"I have news for you. My reputation is bound to suffer the minute anyone gets a good look at me." She regarded her mother warily. "Or do you intend to lock me up here, too, until I do the right thing?"

"Of course not. You're perfectly free to come and go as you like, but I would say a little discretion is called for. You need to think long and hard about how you want to handle all of this. If you're determined not to marry Clint, then you'll have to decide what you're going to tell people, starting with the family."

Angela sighed. "I am not ready to see the family yet." She figured she might not be ready until her baby hit puberty.

"Well, you'd better get ready in a hurry because everyone is coming here tomorrow for our annual pre-Christmas party," her mother retorted, severely cutting into Angela's preferred timetable. "Someone is going to have to explain what's going on."

"I could hide in my room," she said wistfully, but without much hope that her mother would agree to such a cowardly plan.

"And what do you propose I say about Clint?" Her mother's eyes twinkled. "Or were you planning on locking him in here with you?"

"Mother!"

"It is an interesting thought," her mother said, then added slyly, "He is a very handsome man."

"What does that have to do with anything?"

"I imagine that's how you got into this predicament to begin with."

"Mother!"

"Sweetie, he's gorgeous. You're carrying his child. It doesn't take a genius to figure out you were sleeping together."

"I do not want to discuss this with you," she said, flushing with embarrassment.

"OK," her mother said cheerfully. "But I saw something in your eyes when you looked at him that reminded me of another woman."

"Who?" she asked, curious despite the instinct that told her to drop the subject of her very primal and unmistakable reaction to Clint Brady.

"Me. It was exactly the way I used to look when I caught a glimpse of Luke. I could no more help it than I could control the setting of the sun. It was plain as day to anybody who saw me. Jordan and Cody saw it. Luke saw it. Even your natural father was aware of it. I was the only one so deep in denial that I didn't recognize what was happening.''

''My father knew about you and Luke?'' Angela had always wondered about that, but it wasn't something her mother had ever discussed.

''Erik knew how we felt. He also knew we'd never acted on it and that we wouldn't. After he'd had his accident, when he knew he wasn't going to survive, he gave me his blessing. He was an incredible, generous man.'' She brushed away the tears dampening her cheeks, then smiled. ''He would have loved you so much. And he would have been very proud of the gesture you made by studying education the way he always wanted to.''

Neither of them mentioned her failure to follow through and actually go into teaching. ''It seems so strange to me to think that Luke isn't my natural father,'' Angela said instead. ''I've always known it, of course, but on some intellectual level. It never really registered in my heart.''

''Because he's been there literally from the beginning. He adores you.''

''Were he and my father very much alike?''

''Not at all. Your father was the quietest and gentlest of the brothers. He was never suited for ranching, but Harlan bullied him into trying. I'm not sure he's ever entirely forgiven himself for that. If he'd allowed your father to follow his own dream, Erik would never have been on that tractor the day he died.''

She patted Angela's hand. "Enough sad memories for now. You have difficult decisions to make. I have only one word of advice for you."

"Only one?"

"OK, three. Follow your heart."

Angela knew the advice was well meant. She knew it was sound. The only trouble was that the last time she had followed her heart, she had gone and fallen in love with a man who didn't believe in happily ever after.

She knew, too, that even though Clint was trying to bulldoze her into marrying him now, he no more believed in love than he had on the night she'd walked out of his house. It reminded her of some sort of deathbed conversion to religion. Say whatever it took.

She didn't trust the turnaround. She knew better. If anything, Clint's view of love and marriage was probably more jaded now than ever before. He knew that their whole relationship had been built on one huge, gigantic lie. She knew something else, as well, and it terrified her. Clint Brady wasn't the kind of man who'd forgive that kind of betrayal easily. If he was proposing, there was a reason for it, and it for darn sure wasn't love.

Chapter Five

In retrospect, her birthday dinner had been an extremely civilized affair, Angela concluded as she helped Consuela carry the last of the dishes into the kitchen. Clint had even sounded sincere when he'd joined in wishing her a happy birthday.

She smiled grimly. It might have taken him aback if he'd known what she'd wished before she'd tried to blow out the candles on the cake Consuela had baked. Not that it mattered a hoot now. One candle had remained stubbornly lit, so apparently even the gods were in on the conspiracy to keep Clint around.

At any rate, her father and Clint had gotten along better than anyone could have anticipated. They'd spent most of the meal comparing notes on ranching. No blows had been struck. No harsh words had been exchanged.

Every time Angela had been tempted to interrupt or to snap out a sarcastic retort, a warning look from her mother had silenced her. In the end, she'd left the table so frustrated, she'd been ready to spit.

"Your young man—" Consuela began as they entered the kitchen.

"He is not my young man," Angela retorted automatically, hoping to end that particular notion right now.

The housekeeper ignored her. Persistence was as ingrained in Consuela's personality as her smile. She'd had years of dealing with Luke and the other Adams brothers to practice.

"He will make a very good father," she said. Her defiant expression dared Angela to argue with her about that.

"You don't even know him. How can you be certain of a thing like that?"

"Because he treats you well."

"Excuse me? He all but threw me out of his house when I told him I was pregnant."

"No, *niña*," Consuela corrected gently. "I think you ran because you got insulted that he did not react as you wished. That is your way. You run from things rather than facing them, just as you ran from your home years ago."

The hard-truth assessment was a little too accurate, and Consuela did have the proof of Angela's rebellious departure from Texas on her side.

"Whatever," Angela said dismissively. "The point is, a few months ago he didn't even want this baby." Even as she said the words, she rubbed her belly soothingly as if to apologize to the baby for its father's reaction.

"There are many things men do not know they want until we show them," Consuela said. "Lucas could not admit he wanted your mother and you until he almost lost you both. Perhaps it was the same with your Clint."

"*My* Clint is just the kind of man who wants what he can't have. I guarantee you that if I said yes to this crazy wedding nonsense, he would take off before the ceremony."

"Care to test that theory, angel?" a taunting voice inquired from the doorway.

Angela whirled around to find herself face-to-face with the man in question. "I really wish you would stop sneaking up on me."

He grinned. "I came in to see if you and Consuela needed any help cleaning up. You shouldn't be doing dishes on your birthday."

"I thought you and my father were off somewhere discussing breeding or something."

"Breeding is a touchy subject around here these days," he said dryly. "We've been talking about water rights. It's a much safer topic."

"Very funny. I'm so delighted that you two are getting along so famously."

He regarded her with obvious amusement. "You don't sound delighted. You sound miffed. Why is that, I wonder?"

"I don't give two hoots if you and my father become bosom buddies," she said vehemently.

"You sure about that, angel? Weren't you sort of hoping that he'd blow my head off?"

"The prospect did hold a certain appeal, yes," she admitted.

"Niña!" Consuela protested, sketching a cross over her chest. "You should not say such a thing. A lady is always polite to her guests."

"He is not my guest. He's mother's. I didn't want him here, remember?"

Clint grinned at the obviously distraught housekeeper. "I guess the gloves are off."

"Oh, go suck an egg," Angela snapped.

Consuela regarded her with stern disapproval. "That is not the way you were brought up to behave, *niña.*"

She blushed at the rebuke, but she was too angry to let the matter drop. She stared at Consuela in disgust. "For goodness' sakes, isn't anybody around here going to take my side? Clint's been here less than twenty-four hours and everyone is treating him as if he were the prodigal son back from the range wars or something."

"Perhaps we just see what is not so plain to you," Consuela said. "Now go along. I will finish up in here. You two need to talk." She faced Angela. "And to listen," she added pointedly.

Angela sighed.

"Well?" Clint said, when she made no move to do as she'd been told. "Do you feel like going for a walk?"

"Not really," she said stubbornly.

He chuckled, then said, "It's snowing."

Immediately, just as he'd intended, an image of another night filled her head. They had left the bar where they had met and walked aimlessly through the small Montana town of Rocky Ridge. They had said little as they strolled along, thrilling to new sensations and content merely to have hands clasped. They had walked for an hour or more, both of them afraid to break the spell of unexpected intimacy that had captivated them.

Clearly uncertain of where things would go from there, Clint had walked her back to her car. Standing there, his hands on her waist, he had bent his head oh, so slowly and kissed her. It had been the sweetest, most innocent of kisses, but it had been the start of something incendiary.

As he pulled away, his eyes locked with hers, and she had felt the delicate touch of something cold and damp against her cheek. A snowflake. It had melted against her heated flesh practically before she realized what it was. It took another and another before it had registered.

"It's snowing," she had whispered, delighted, her face turned up toward the sky.

"Nothing's more beautiful than sitting in front of a fire and watching the snow fall outside," Clint had said. "Would you like to share that with me?"

The answer had been easy and as inevitable as that kiss. By dawn, in front of a blazing fire, they had become lovers. And outside, the ground had been covered with the first snow of the season, a fairy-tale dusting of white that had turned the world into a wonderland.

There had been more snow that winter, blizzards, in fact, but none had been as memorable as the one that had fallen on that first night she had spent in Clint's arms.

She gazed into his eyes now and saw that he was daring her to recapture that magic.

"I'll get my coat," she said quietly and started from the kitchen. She turned back, still defiant, but a little sad. "It won't be the same, you know."

His lips curved at her tone. "Maybe not," he agreed. "Maybe it will be better."

"Are you warm enough?" Clint asked. The minute they'd gotten outside, he'd started wondering if he'd made yet another foolish mistake dragging Angela out on such a bitter cold night. When he'd noticed the snow falling, it had taken him back to another time, another place, when things between them had been far less complicated. That night had been about discovery and beginnings. Perhaps tonight would be about a new beginning for the two of them, one built on a more solid foundation.

"I'm fine," she insisted yet again, her face turned up to the sky.

Snowflakes landed on her cheeks and melted in rapid succession. They caught in her eyelashes. She looked as ecstatic and as shatteringly vulnerable as if they had just made love. Clint wanted to kiss her so badly his body ached. He forced himself to hold back. Kissing had been the start of their problems. It wouldn't solve them. As the feisty Consuela had insisted, they needed to talk more than anything else at the moment. Unfortunately he had no idea where to begin. The emotions ripping through him were complex and conflicting.

He could start with his outrage over her running off. Or he could yell about the risks she'd taken traveling alone, especially these last couple of weeks with the baby almost due. Or he could demand an explanation for the monumental lie that stood between them. That last angered him more every time he thought about it.

Hattie Jones, indeed! Had she merely plucked the name out of the air on the spur of the moment? He imagined that more than one woman meeting a man for the first time in a bar might fib about her identity until she knew precisely with whom she was dealing. But wouldn't an honest woman come clean when the flirtation turned into a relationship? Why in hell had Angela perpetuated the lie until the day she'd left him? He had the feeling that any answer she had for that would only infuriate him more, would perhaps deepen his disdain beyond repair.

"Go on," she said, breaking the silence.

He regarded her blankly. "What?"

"Yell at me. Tell me what an idiot I was to run away. Tell me what a jerk I was for pretending to be Hattie Jones for all those months."

"I'm the one who feels like a jerk," he grumbled, hitting on what galled him most, his own stupidity. "Why didn't I see that you were lying?"

"What man would suspect that a woman he'd been sleeping with for the better part of a year wasn't who she'd claimed to be?" she retorted. "I wanted

you to think of me as Hattie Jones. I wanted to be
Hattie Jones, at least for a while.''

"I just have one question, why? Why did you lie?
Not that first night, but later. Why did you keep lying?''

For a minute he thought he was going to get a flip
response, some quick and easy explanation that
would diminish the magnitude of what she'd done.
Instead, her expression turned thoughtful and the silence dragged on. He let it.

"I suppose I just wanted a chance to be somebody
else," she said eventually.

He stared at her in amazement. "Why? What on
earth was wrong with being Angela Adams?"

She closed her eyes and sighed. "I know it doesn't
make any sense to you. Just look around. I grew up
on an incredible ranch. My parents are the best.
There was no possible way on earth for me to be
dissatisfied, right?''

"But you obviously were," he said, trying to
make sense of it. He would have given anything to
have grown up in a place like this with a family like
hers.

Instead, he'd had to scramble for every penny he'd
earned. His dream of owning his own spread had
seemed impossible once. He had made it happen. He
didn't resent the difficulties he'd faced or the com-
parative ease of her past. It was just the way life was.
A man could let it make him bitter or make him
strong. He'd opted long ago for strong.

He saw that she was still struggling to put her
thoughts into words and conceded that even though

none of what she was saying made any sense to him, she was genuinely troubled. There was no mistaking that.

"Not dissatisfied," she said finally. "I felt smothered. There's a whole long story about how I was born, right here in Luke's bedroom, as a matter of fact. Luke isn't my natural father. His brother was."

Clint tried to hide his shock, but failed. The relationships here at least had seemed so straightforward, but obviously they were anything but. She shrugged.

"It's complicated," she said in what was an apparent understatement. "Anyway, everyone credits my birth with getting Luke and my mother together. I was supposed to be some sort of Christmas blessing."

She held out her hand and caught a snowflake, watching it melt before she spoke again. "It's weird growing up as part of some sort of family legend. I always felt as if so much was expected of me. The truth was, no matter how hard I tried, I would always be mortal, just another human being with lots and lots of flaws, when I was supposed to be an angel. Maybe if I'd had sisters named Faith, Hope and Charity, the pressure wouldn't have seemed so intense."

Clint chuckled, even though he could see that she was half-serious. He'd had six brothers and two sisters. The pressures she'd felt as an only child were an enigma to him.

"Don't laugh," she said. "Just being born an Adams comes with all sorts of baggage. Grandpa Harlan figures because we carry the name, we're all destined for something important. He also figures he gets to decide what that will be. Just ask Luke. He was the first one to rebel. Then Jordan. Even Cody bolted for a while. Only my dad tried to please him by going along with Grandpa Harlan's divine plan. It killed him.''

Clint was stunned by her words. "Killed him? How?''

"Granddad wanted him to be a rancher, so he tried, when what he really wanted to do was teach. He was always distracted. His head was always in some book. You know yourself, a rancher can't afford to be distracted. Too many things can happen in the blink of an eye. Who knows what he was thinking about, but the tractor he was riding here on Luke's ranch ran into a ditch and overturned. He died a few hours later.''

She sighed sadly. "You would have thought Grandpa Harlan would learn from his mistake, but he's still as meddlesome and controlling as he ever was. So is Luke. They are the most wonderful, best-intentioned men in the universe, but I couldn't breathe under the weight of all those expectations.''

"So you ran off and became Hattie Jones,'' Clint surmised. He'd heard of people moving, settling in someplace new to reinvent themselves, but a whole new name and identity? Wasn't that carrying it a little too far?

"Not at first. Actually, other than choosing Stanford instead of the University of Texas, my first act of rebellion was relatively mild. I studied English lit and education, instead of agriculture.''

She smiled briefly. It seemed a little wistful to him.

"I meant to be the teacher my father had wanted to be," she added. "I messed up at that, too. I graduated from college by the skin of my teeth, applied for my first teaching job and got cold feet. I knew in my gut I had no business at all being in a classroom trying to shape little minds, not when my own was such a mess."

"Is that when you came to Montana?"

She nodded. "Rocky Ridge was the first town I'd driven through that appealed to me. When you see Los Pinos, I think you'll understand why. Ironically, the two places are very much alike. Anyway, I walked into that bar on pure impulse to apply for the waitressing job posted in the window and there you were. It wasn't just that you were the sexiest thing I'd ever laid eyes on. You looked dangerous, harder and tougher than the men I'd met at school certainly."

She reached up and touched his hair. "All that shaggy, sun-streaked hair and those devilish blue eyes. You were flirting outrageously with me, and I felt as if you were my first and best chance to be a whole new person, a woman who was exciting and sensual and wicked. With you I could be anybody I wanted to be."

Clint wasn't sure why, but the explanation chilled him. He didn't want to be anyone's act of rebellion. People who stuck together ought to bring out the best in one another, not the worst.

"I'm glad I could oblige," he said with a surprising edge of bitterness. "You played the game well. Hattie was a real sexy invention. We had some good times."

She frowned ever so slightly at his words. "You say that as if the good times were all in the past."

"I think maybe they were," he said slowly. He gazed into her eyes, searching for the woman who had once intrigued him so. A man would have to be a fool to try to perpetuate something that had only been make-believe. Sometimes it was smarter just to concede that the game was over and call it a draw.

"What are you saying?" she demanded.

It appeared to him that there was a touch of panic in her voice. A day ago that might have delighted him. Now it hardly seemed to matter.

He wanted to tell her that coming here was a mistake, that trying to convince her to marry him was a mistake, but that would ruin his long-range plan for getting custody of his child. "Just that you can't recapture the past," he said instead. "I thought you could, but I was wrong."

Her eyes darkened with hurt, but he noticed she didn't try to argue with him.

"Then you'll be leaving, after all?"

He thought he detected a blending of hope and despair in her voice, but he was too upset to figure out what was going on in that mixed-up mind of hers. He shook his head. "Not a chance, sweetheart. I meant what I said about that wedding. That baby of ours is going to have my name."

"Why? You can't possibly care about the child of a woman you despise."

Despise was too strong a word, but he didn't correct her. "I care about *my* child, though. Make no mistake about it, angel, this baby is mine."

Now there was no mistaking the genuine panic in her expression. "Meaning?"

"I will fight you for him," he declared, then amended, "or her."

He saw her shudder as the words registered and knew he had shown his hand too soon. He regretted that, but it wouldn't change anything. Maybe the fight would be fairer if they both knew where they stood. Fairness was a lot more than she deserved.

"You can't," she protested.

"Watch me," he said and walked away.

"You can't win," she shouted after him. "Not here. The Adams name means something here in Texas."

"And Jones?" he taunted. "Does the name Hattie Jones mean anything?"

That silenced her. He was halfway back up the lane toward the house when he heard the rustle of her coat against denim, the crunch of ice beneath her boots as she followed him. He wasn't sure why, but he waited for her at the door.

That was a mistake, he realized at once, when he saw the sheen of tears on her cheeks. Then he told himself that the dampness was merely snowflakes melting. A woman as coldly calculating as Hattie Jones—or Angela Adams—couldn't possibly be crying.

Angela was holding back sobs by the time she closed the door to her room behind her. She would not let Clint Brady see that he had hurt her. She would not let him see that she was terrified of his threat to take the baby. But behind that closed door, she let her fear and anguish flow unchecked. Still in her coat, damp now with snow, she huddled on her bed, clutching a pillow. She had botched things again. She had tried to be open and honest with Clint—albeit belatedly—and he had taken her words and twisted them into something ugly.

He would use them against her, if he had to. She had seen that much in his hard expression. She had watched his pride kick in and she had shuddered. Months ago she had seen that his pride was a more than even match for any Adams.

She knew exactly what would happen. He would go into court and portray her as a woman unfit to be a mother, a woman who had committed the ultimate betrayal by pretending to be someone else entirely. He would describe her behavior in Montana as something wanton and sinful and she would be helpless to deny it, because that was exactly what she had meant it to be. Hattie Jones had been outrageous and deceptive, because those were traits that Angela Adams had been forbidden in her nice, protected world.

What had she been thinking? That wasn't who she was, not really. Just look how quickly she had done the traditional thing and fallen in love with the man. Just look at the perfectly normal expectation she'd had back then that they would get married and raise the baby they'd conceived in love together.

In the end she'd even messed up being outrageous. Now everyone was going to know about her foolish mistake. Her parents. Grandpa Harlan. The whole damned world, if Clint had his way. She couldn't let that happen. She had to find some way to compromise with him, some way to win him back. She had to smooth things over until tempers cooled.

Only a few hours ago he'd been determined to marry her. He'd wanted the baby to have his name. Obviously he wanted to do things the traditional way, just as she had from the very moment she'd discovered she was pregnant with his child. He wanted to behave honorably, because down deep that was the kind of man Clint Brady was. She had recognized that in him from the beginning. Maybe it was why she had felt so free to behave as she had, because she had known she could trust him not to harm her in any way.

He'd never taken back his proposal, not even when his temper had flared. Maybe his motives weren't as innocent and pure as he had wanted everyone else to believe, but he hadn't retracted the words. She could use that to her advantage.

She got slowly out of bed and changed into her nightgown. She washed away the last traces of her tears. There would be no more, she resolved.

She smiled at herself in the mirror. She had learned a few tricks as Hattie Jones. It was time she made them pay off for her. Once, Clint hadn't been able to resist her. Whatever her name, she was still that same woman.

Before anyone knew that his interest in marriage was totally self-serving, she was going to make absolutely certain that they were walking down the aisle. She was going to protect her role in her baby's life…no matter what Clint had in mind for the future.

Chapter Six

"So, where's my precious angel!"

Angela heard her grandfather's booming voice all the way upstairs and sighed.

"Not yet, please God," she whispered. She wasn't ready to see him yet, wasn't prepared to see even a hint of judgment in his eyes. She wasn't ready to explain the baby she was expecting. She certainly wasn't prepared to explain Clint, not with things so terribly unsettled between them.

Nor could she rely on her parents to smooth the way. It wouldn't be fair to expect them to give answers to so many difficult questions, when she didn't know the answers herself.

"Not yet," she pleaded again.

Apparently God had other ideas. She heard her grandfather's two-at-a-time tread on the steps, then the sharp, impatient rap of his knuckles against her door.

"You in there, darlin'?"

Resigned to the inevitable, she drew in a deep breath, plastered a bright smile on her face and threw open the door.

"Grandpa," she said and felt herself scooped into an awkward, but exuberant bear hug.

After a minute he set her back on her feet and stepped back. "Let me get a good look at you." His gaze traveled over her mound of a belly, then came to rest on her face. His eyes were troubled, but his beaming smile never faltered.

"You look pretty as a picture," he declared. "Impending motherhood obviously agrees with you."

"You should have seen me the first month," she said, thinking of the nausea that had been a constant companion. There had been mornings she hadn't wanted to budge from bed, much less see herself in a mirror.

"I wish I had," he said at once, "instead of you being away in who-knows-where all by yourself."

Sensing the likelihood that a lecture was about to begin, she hurriedly said, "My turn now."

She quickly scanned him from head to toe. Other than a few more gray hairs and a slight stoop to his shoulders he looked as fit as ever. He was one of those men who wore his age well and would until his nineties, God willing. He was almost in his eighties now and barely looked sixty.

"You haven't changed a bit," she told him.

"You're every bit as handsome as you were the day I left."

He winked at her. "Love," he confided. "I highly recommend it at any age."

Angela grinned at the allusion to the woman who'd turned his whole outlook on life upside down. "How is Janet?" she asked.

"Perfect. Wonderful," he enthused, eyes sparkling at the thought of her. "She's downstairs with your mama. She's as anxious to see you as I was, but she shows more restraint. She still says I haven't got a lick of patience or any understanding whatsoever of privacy."

Angela grinned at him. "I guess there are some traits not even love can change. Not in an Adams man, anyway."

His expression sobered. "So when are you going to make me a great-granddaddy?"

"The way I feel right now, it can't be soon enough. Another week or two is what the doctor told me before I left Seattle to come home."

He shook his head. "I can't believe it. Me with a child in her teens and a great-grandbaby on the way. Talk about a couple of curve balls. Life's thrown me some doozies. Not that I'm complaining. I wouldn't have it any other way."

She grinned at his expression of delighted disbelief. "How are my cousins?" she asked, referring not only to the teenager her grandfather and Janet had had together, but to Janet's daughter Jenny. It was Jenny's theft of Grandpa Harlan's truck that had brought them together in the first place. As a child,

Angela had always thought Jenny's rebellious ways fascinating. She'd envied the daring teenager. In the end, it appeared she'd outdone her.

"Jenny's going to be teaching school soon," he said proudly, apparently oblivious to the irony. If his reaction to Erik's desires had been half so approving, perhaps Angela's natural father still would have been alive.

"As for Lizzy," he went on, "she is the most beautiful child ever born and the smartest."

"Don't you let Luke, Cody and Jordan hear you say that," Angela chided. "You'll hurt their feelings. They all think they were gorgeous and sexy from day one."

"Those three have hides like an elephant," he said dismissively. "My talk's not going to faze them. Besides, they were never as cute as Lizzy. She's her daddy's girl. Top of her class every year."

Amused by his bragging, she teased, "Don't you suppose just maybe she inherited some of her intelligence from her mother? Janet is an attorney, after all, and a very good one." In fact, Janet Runningbear Adams had built a national reputation for her work on behalf of Native American causes.

He grinned. "Much as it galls me, I suppose I can share some of the credit with her." He looped an arm around Angela's shoulders. "Come on down and see them. Jenny's not here yet, but the others are waiting. Lizzy was ecstatic when we told her about the baby. She's tired of being the youngest. Cody and Jordan should be turning up soon with their broods. You won't believe how grown-up all my grandbabies are."

The thought of facing them all made her palms sweat. Overwhelming uncles, rock-steady aunts and rambunctious cousins. It promised to be too much.

"You go on ahead," she suggested. "I'm not quite ready."

Ignoring her hesitance, he declared, "You look fine to me. Another touch of powder on your nose isn't going to make you one bit prettier."

"It's not that. I..." She gazed into his eyes, pleading with him to understand.

His expression softened at once. "You're scared, aren't you?" he said bluntly. "Or ashamed. Which is it?"

When she said nothing, he captured her face between his work-roughened hands and met her gaze evenly. "Darling girl, there's no need to be. Family's all that's important to us. Everyone here has made more than their share of mistakes. Everyone here loves you, no matter what. Don't you know that by now? All that matters to us is that you're home again."

She nodded, tears welling up. Maybe it was his words, maybe her wacky hormones, but she felt like bawling. "I'll be there in a few minutes, I promise. I'm not going to duck out the back door."

His eyes twinkled. "What about that tree by your bedroom window? You thinking of climbing down that the way you did when you were a girl so you could sneak off to see your friends?"

She laughed at the memory, as well as the impossibility of resorting to such an escape now. She patted her belly. "Like this? I don't think so. I'll be down to face the music, and I'll use the stairs like a proper, grown-up lady."

"You'd feel braver with me by your side," he said lightly. "Nobody's going to mess with my darlin' girl with me around."

She grinned at that. "You can't protect me from everything, Grandpa."

"I can sure as hell try," he said fiercely. "I love you, angel. Don't make any mistake about that."

She stood on tiptoe and kissed his weathered cheek. "I love you, too. And I didn't realize until now just how much I'd missed you."

He cast one last worried look in her direction, then retreated downstairs. Angela stared after him for what seemed an eternity, trying to work up the courage to join everyone.

"Facing your family's harder than you expected, isn't it?" Clint said, exiting the guest room across the hall.

"Is it necessary for you to spy on me?" she snapped, then recalled that she was supposed to be trying to win the man back, not offend him. "Sorry. It's just that seeing Grandpa Harlan shook me more than I'd expected it to. He acts as if I haven't done anything wrong, when I know perfectly well he must be furious."

"More likely with me than with you," Clint suggested. "Want to go downstairs with me and protect me?"

She glanced up at him with astonishment and saw

the sympathy and understanding in his eyes. She knew perfectly well he wasn't one bit terrified of her grandfather or any man. Despite their battle the night before, he was offering her his support. She thought she had never loved him more than she did at this moment. It really was too bad that everything between them had gotten so messed up. At heart he was a decent, sensitive man. Maybe if she'd remembered that and given him time to adjust to the idea of being a daddy, things would never have gotten so out of hand.

For just a moment she allowed herself to imagine the way it could have been. Arriving home as Clint's wife, their first baby on the way, would have turned the holidays into something unforgettable.

Instead, there was bound to be an endless amount of tension and strain as everyone tiptoed around the subject of their relationship. She didn't envy Clint his role as an outsider, not with everyone bound to feel especially protective of her. He had no idea what he had let himself in for by accepting her mother's invitation to stay on through the holidays.

"I wonder if he knows yet that you're here," she murmured thoughtfully.

"I doubt it. I haven't heard any explosions since he arrived, have you?"

"My father might have warned him."

"Oh, somehow I doubt that," he said with a wry expression. "Your father would probably be delighted if your grandfather took one look at me and ripped me to shreds. Luke can't do it himself because we declared a truce yesterday."

She studied him curiously. "I wondered about that. How did you win him over?"

"I didn't say I'd won him over, just that we'd agreed not to brawl. I'm on probation. He's waiting for me to make just one tiny mistake and then, I guarantee it will be his pleasure to chase me all the way back to Montana."

She regarded him impishly. "One tiny mistake, huh?"

He scowled at her. "Don't go getting any ideas, angel. I have no intention of treading on anyone's toes until I can claim my child."

She ignored the subtle reminder of his threat. She would deal with that when the time came. Instead, some thoroughly outrageous instinct, probably left from her days as Hattie, made her link her arm through his. Now was as good a time as any to start her scheme to win him back.

"Let's go," she said with a wink. "Let's see just how much trouble I can get you into, if I try."

There wasn't so much as a twinkle in his eyes when he met her gaze evenly. "That works both ways, sweetheart. You'd do well to remember that."

The deliberate taunt jangled her nerves, just as he'd obviously intended. It reminded her that she was playing games with a master.

At the top of the stairs, before Clint's quick retort had evened the score, her promise of troublemaking had seemed like a fine idea. She'd expected to sail into the midst of her family with restored confidence.

Instead, standing in the doorway to the living room with a circle of inquisitive faces staring at them, she realized she'd miscalculated. Walking into that room on Clint's arm hadn't been the masterstroke she'd anticipated. It had simply quadrupled the speculation and added to the pressure. Now it wouldn't be just her folks and Consuela anticipating a wedding, but this whole roomful of relatives. Why hadn't she seen that she should have locked the man in a closet until after New Year's?

Since she couldn't seem to find her tongue, it was Clint who worked his way around the group, introducing himself with an ease that she found thoroughly annoying. Why wasn't he feeling the same kind of intimidation that she felt? This was her family, after all. Right this second he seemed more at home than she did.

He slowed when he got to her grandfather. She saw the two men taking each other's measure. Everyone seemed to be holding their collective breath, waiting to see what Harlan Adams would do or say to the man who had gotten his grandchild into the fix she was in.

Her grandfather's expression was unreadable, but he was the first to hold out his hand. "Welcome, son. It's good to have you with us for the holidays."

The palpable tension in the room eased.

"Thank you, sir," Clint said with just the right amount of deference. "I've heard quite a lot about you. It's a pleasure to meet you at last."

Who's lying now? Angela thought bitterly. Up until the day before yesterday, Clint Brady hadn't even known this family existed, yet he was treating them all as if they were people he genuinely cared about getting to know.

Worse, they were falling for it, toppling like dominoes under the warmth of his natural charm.

She sighed and tried to be grateful for the fact that his presence had shifted some of the attention away from her for the moment. She was able to slip from the room and head for the kitchen to get her bearings before yet another carload of exuberant Adamses showed up.

She was surprised to find the kitchen deserted. There was no sign of Consuela, even though preparations for that night's feast were well underway. Expecting the housekeeper to return at any second, she filled a glass with milk and sank down into a chair at the table where she had spent many an afternoon as a girl talking out her problems, sometimes with Consuela, just as often with her mother. This room had heard a lot of secrets over the years.

When the door swung open, she glanced up and saw that it was her step-grandmother who'd followed her. Angela's smile was genuine as she surveyed the tall, slim woman with the shoulder-length black hair and sparkling brown eyes. She had always admired the strong, feisty lawyer who'd stolen her grandfather's heart. Janet Runningbear Adams exuded the kind of quiet serenity Angela wished she could attain. It had taken a woman with amazing self-confidence to stand up to Harlan Adams strong will and become his partner in life, as well as his mate.

Janet rested a hand on her shoulder, when Angela would have risen to hug her. "Stay where you are.

I know how difficult it is to get up and down at this stage of pregnancy. Are you feeling OK?''

"As well as any blimp could be expected to feel,'' Angela told her. "Did you come in here looking for Consuela? Or a snack, maybe?''

"Actually I came to see you.''

"Oh?''

"It was your grandfather's idea that we have a talk. He got it into his head last night after he spoke to your father and heard that Clint was here. Naturally he practically shoved me out of the living room just now, instead of letting me wait a bit.''

Angela regarded her warily. "What did he want you to talk to me about?''

"He thought you might need some legal protection.''

"Legal protection? From Clint? You mean like a restraining order or something?''

Her incredulity made Janet smile. "Actually, I think he was thinking more along the lines of a prenuptial agreement.''

"Oh.'' Given the lack of real wedding plans and her own financial circumstances, the idea struck her as just as ludicrous. Besides, she'd always thought that starting a marriage by figuring out the financial ins and outs of ending it showed a certain lack of faith in the relationship.

"Why on earth would he think I needed something like that?''

"I'm not recommending it,'' Janet said hastily, clearly reacting to the defensive note in Angela's voice. "Your grandfather and I had quite a few words over that very subject when we got married. We ripped up a lot of paper, but a prenuptial agreement does serve a purpose. It can protect what's yours or his."

"You may not have noticed, but I don't have a lot," Angela said dryly. "My savings account is virtually empty. So's my checkbook. As for Clint, his ranch is hardly the kind of place that needs protecting from my greedy little grasp."

"But you're an Adams," Janet reminded her as if that alone explained the need for such an agreement.

"He's hardly likely to try to steal my name."

Janet grimned. "No, but you stand to inherit this ranch. You have a sizable trust fund from your grandfather that will be yours in another couple of years."

Neither of those things had ever crossed her mind, maybe because she'd figured her parents and grandfather would live forever. "Clint not only doesn't know about that, he wouldn't care if he did," she said with absolute certainty.

"Are you so sure? I was under the impression that there was a time when he wasn't the least bit interested in marrying you or claiming his baby. Now he turns up here and does a one-eighty. Maybe that's honestly motivated," Janet said reasonably. "Maybe not, but you ought to be sure before you risk everything that will one day be yours."

Angela shuddered. "I don't know. That seems so cold and calculating. It's not like Clint at all. Besides, none of this ever mattered to me, anyway."

"Possibly not, but you should think about this

baby you're carrying. You should protect what's yours for your child's future. Will you at least consider what I've said?"

Angela nodded reluctantly. Janet reached across the table and squeezed her hand. "If there's anything else you need to talk about, I'm available, not as a lawyer, but as a friend. Remember that. Sometimes it takes an objective outsider to help sort things out."

"You're hardly an outsider," she reminded her.

"I wasn't born an Adams," Janet said wryly. "In the end it makes a difference. An Adams is single-minded when it comes to family. On occasion I have to remind Harlan that there are two sides to most stories."

Angela grinned. "I imagine you do. Thank you. Maybe one of these days when I figure out what all the questions are, I'll see if you have any answers."

"Bottom line? There's really only one question and I think you already know what that is."

Angela sighed. "Do we love each other, I suppose."

"That's the one."

"Any insights?" Angela asked wistfully.

"I haven't seen the two of you in the same room long enough to tell yet." She winked. "Give me until tomorrow. I'll share my matchmaking insights with you, though to hear Jenny tell it, I'm really lousy at it."

That said, she left Angela alone again with her thoughts. All of the things she had to consider were beginning to give her a headache. If she'd thought she could manage it without getting caught, she would have slipped back up to her room and hidden out there until the holidays were over.

The distrust between her and Clint had just escalated to another level, fueled by Janet's suggestions that he had somehow discovered her potential net worth and decided that maybe being married wouldn't be so terrible after all.

At this rate, would they ever be able to rediscover the feelings that had drawn them together so many months ago? Or were they destined always to be at cross-purposes, always trying to second-guess motives?

Angela sighed heavily. She'd been exposed to a lot of very strong marriages over her lifetime. Jordan and Kelly, Cody and Melissa, her own parents, Grandpa Harlan and Janet. All of them had shown her the power of love. She believed in it with all her heart. She also knew that trust was at the core of each and every one of them.

Over the last few days the seeds of distrust had been sown between her and Clint, intentionally or inadvertently. It didn't really matter which. The point was, could any couple overcome that kind of obstacle? The sad answer, it seemed to her, was no.

Clint knew he was on display. Hell, he was on trial. So far he thought he'd managed to hold his own. Harlan Adams was an even tougher nut to crack than his son, but Clint thought he seemed at least willing to wait and see if Clint could prove himself worthy of an Adams.

The irony of it all wasn't lost on him. If he'd

known everything he knew now about her family on the day he'd met Angela, even he would have said he was out of his league. But he hadn't fallen for Angela Adams. He'd been caught up in a blazing romance with Hattie Jones, whose background had been kept a mystery and whose heart was as generous as any woman's on earth.

That was what made him crazy now. He kept remembering all of Hattie's best traits and questioning which of them existed in Angela. Had any man ever been presented with such a complex puzzle to sort out? If so, he'd like to meet him and discover how he'd done it without losing his sanity in the process.

When another carload of family members turned up—Cody and Melissa and their kids, if he'd gotten the names straight—he took the opportunity to slip away from the ensuing chaos and hunt for Angela. She'd vanished again, though he was pretty sure this time that she'd gone no farther than the kitchen. He'd noticed that she seemed to retreat there an awful lot. It must have always been some sort of haven for her. That suited him just fine, since the warm room and the sympathetic housekeeper drew him, as well.

Sure enough, Angela was sitting at the table, eyes closed, a half-empty glass of milk on the table, her feet propped up on another chair. He noticed that her ankles were swollen. Since she was either asleep or simply oblivious to his arrival, he slid into the chair closest to her feet and lifted them into his lap. He massaged them gently, regretting all the exhausting days she must have spent when he hadn't been around to perform this simple act of kindness for her.

Her sigh of pure pleasure sounded genuine. Slowly she opened her eyes and stared at him in surprise. "You?"

"Who'd you think it was?" he inquired, chuckling at her disconcerted expression.

"I don't know. Consuela maybe."

"I'm disappointed, angel. I thought for sure you'd recognize my touch."

"It's been a long time." Her gaze caught his and lingered. "A very long time."

"Some things a man never forgets," he said. "I guess it's different for a woman."

"Not really," she admitted softly.

The response and the hint of intimacy hovered in the air between them, too fragile to test. Clint was wise enough for once to keep silent. He contented himself with the sighs his ongoing massage earned him.

"I suppose I can't put it off any longer," she said eventually.

"What?"

"Joining the others."

"There are more here now," he advised her. "Your uncle Cody, I believe. I skipped out before meeting him and came to look for you."

She grinned. "Two Adams men didn't alarm you, but three began to seem like impressive odds, I guess."

"Something like that." He gave her a lazy smile. "Or maybe I just missed you."

"I wish I could believe that," she said almost wistfully.

"Then do. It's true."

She regarded him with blatant skepticism. "True or convenient," she muttered.

His fingers stilled against her soft skin. "Convenient?" he asked, his tone lethal.

There was a flash of pure panic in her eyes, but it quickly gave way to defiance. "Yes, convenient," she said firmly. "You're up to something, Clint Brady. There's not a doubt in my mind about that."

"Sweetheart, unlike you, I laid all my cards out on the table. I intend to marry you and give my child my name."

"And then?" she asked distrustfully.

"Well, I suppose we'll just have to take things as they come after that."

She scowled. "Now that's the part that has me worried."

"It shouldn't." He slid his hand up her leg, beneath her slacks. The skin was soft as silk and warmed to his caress. "We were always very, very good at improvising."

An obviously reluctant smile tugged at her lips. "Yes," she conceded eventually. "Yes, we were."

Chapter Seven

Clint had grown up in what he considered to be a large family, plenty of brothers and sisters to make holidays chaotic, if stressful, even a handful of cousins on his mother's side to fill up the house. He'd always thought that was one reason he'd moved to such a small town in Montana and chosen an isolated ranch. He'd longed for some peace and quiet.

He now knew with absolute certainty that the one thing he would never get with Angela in his life was peace and quiet, not on holidays spent in Texas, anyway.

By three in the afternoon he'd lost count of the number of people who'd arrived for the pre-Christmas party. Harlan Adams presided over the celebration with as much pride as any clan patriarch in a state filled with larger-than-life men. He commanded the respect not only of his sons, but his daughters-in-law and of all the grandchildren. They deferred to him in most matters, teased him unmercifully about others and always, always showed their love with every word and action.

Clint knew it took an incredible man to earn so much adoration. He'd never had a male role model of his own. He'd thought when he first met Luke Adams that Luke might be the man to emulate. Now he realized that Luke was simply his father's son: a strong, honest man shaped by a strong, honest father. Cody and Jordan were, as well. Parenting such fine men was a legacy Harlan Adams could be proud of.

Watching their interaction made Clint feel the kind of gut-deep envy that he'd never before experienced as child or adult. Sure, as a kid he'd wanted a dad around for the simple stuff, a father-son dinner at school, a game of catch in the backyard, an afternoon of fishing. He'd regretted not having something that even his own brothers and sisters had experienced. But he hadn't felt this wrenching sense of having missed something powerful and meaningful in his life.

He had no idea what kind of man his father had become when he'd left them, but the fact that he'd gone said quite a lot about his character. It was obvious to Clint that his father hadn't come from the same sort of stock that Harlan Adams had. Even if he'd stayed, his influence on Clint's life probably wouldn't have been as sharply defined as Harlan Adams's had been on his sons.

It was rare for Clint to feel that he wasn't another

man's equal, but in this crowd he began to have his doubts. His own code of ethics was decent, his own brand of loyalty deep, but he wasn't at all sure it measured up to what he was witnessing at this family gathering.

Having doubts about himself always made him edgy. As a kid he'd taken swings at anyone who'd suggested he was less than they were. As an adult he'd learned to avoid situations that would put him at a disadvantage.

Now, feeling decidedly edgy, he retreated outside after Consuela's gargantuan feast. He figured it would be hours before anyone even noticed he'd gone. If they did notice, they'd probably be relieved since his presence had created more than one awkward, stressful moment.

Angela surely wouldn't miss him. She was finally and totally caught up in her reunion with her family, just as she should be. Whatever questions anyone had raised had been silenced, probably by stern admonitions from on high. In the absence of such probing, she had relaxed. Her smile had come more frequently, twisting his insides with the innocent beauty of it. He thought she looked happier than he'd ever made her. That made him edgy, too.

"Too overwhelming?" she asked, suddenly appearing at his side as if he'd conjured her up. Her hair was whipping around her face in the icy wind. That same wind had put patches of color in her cheeks. She was desperately tugging at her coat, trying to close the ever-widening gap over her expanding tummy, but it was a losing battle.

He smiled at the futile effort and drew a responding scowl.

"You try adding an inch a day to your waistline and see how long clothes fit," she grumbled.

"You shouldn't be out here," he said curtly. "The sun's about to go down and the temperature's dropping."

"I needed some air and a chance to let my face muscles relax."

He grinned at that. He'd felt much the same way himself. Still, he couldn't resist the urge to taunt. "Too much smiling?" he inquired. "Didn't I read somewhere that it takes fewer muscles to smile than it does to frown?"

She chuckled. "Have you been reading those beauty magazines I left behind?"

It was closer to the truth than he wanted to admit. She'd cluttered the whole darn ranch house with her romance novels and her magazines. After she'd gone, he'd felt closer to her when he'd glanced through them. Silly nonsense, for the most part, at least when it came to the magazines.

The books had been another story. Some of those writers could weave a fascinating story, and the steamy sex in a few of them had left him downright hot for days afterward. He'd regretted not peeking at them when Hattie had been around to satisfy the urges they stirred.

"You have, haven't you?" she demanded, laughing. "I don't believe it."

He feigned a scowl. "Don't let it get around, an-gel. You'll ruin my reputation."

She eyed him speculatively and he could see evidence of the insatiable Hattie in her expression. She had always been as eager as he to make love, as anxious as he for a stolen caress or a passionate kiss.

"Exactly what other tidbits of useful information did you pick up from your reading?" she asked.

Suddenly enjoying the game, he reached over and tucked a wayward curl behind her ear. He lingered to trace his thumb across her lower lip and felt the shock of his touch jolt through her. The flare of yearning in her eyes was unmistakable. Once upon a time he'd seen it often. That kind of longing was heady stuff for a man who'd always been odd man out with his own family. To have someone want him so desperately fueled his masculine ego and filled his heart. Only after she'd gone had he realized just how much he'd come to depend on it. Now she was openly offering him a chance to grab just a small taste of what they'd once shared.

"For starters," he said quietly, his gaze pinned on hers, "I learned that sometimes a kiss is more devastating than sex, that the brush of a finger across a woman's lips can make her toes curl." He studied her quizzically as he suited action to words. "Is it true, angel?"

She swallowed hard, but never took her eyes from his. The bold look further inflamed him as he waited to see if she'd respond honestly or lie.

"It seems to be," she said. "But I think one experiment is hardly scientific."

Smiling to himself, he traced the outline of her mouth, lingering at the dip in the top lip, then skimming the bottom lip lightly with his fingernail. She trembled.

"Two for two," he said with satisfaction. "Enough yet?"

"Not nearly enough," she insisted.

"The experimenting's getting dangerous," he warned.

"You scared?" she taunted.

"No, but maybe you should be."

"Nothing scares an Adams," she retorted.

He laughed. "That's definitely one part of your heritage you never denied. You were always game for any risk."

"So were you. Some said it was what made us a good match," she said.

"Still feeling intrepid?"

"Always."

He slowly lowered his head until his mouth hovered over hers. "Still?"

With her gaze pinned to his, she simply nodded.

The touch of their lips set off a familiar blazing heat. Clint was no longer aware of the biting cold of the wind. Inside, his body temperature shot up. Perspiration broke out on his brow.

When Ángela settled into his embrace, her lips molded to his, he felt as if he could strip naked, make love to her right here and right now, and never even notice the frozen ground beneath them. She could make him hotter faster than a wood stove set on high. Always could.

"Hey, Justin, is there steam rising from Angie?"

Reality slammed into him at the comment. Angela

went absolutely still in his arms. He guessed the whispered question came from young Harlan Patrick, Cody's son. He was twenty or so and had a smart mouth and a young man's fascination with sex. That much had been evident from the moment he arrived.

"Maybe we should douse them with water," Jordan's son, Justin, whispered back. "That's what Dad does to the cats when he catches them going at it."

"You do and you are going to be two very uncomfortable young men for the rest of your visit," Clint said. Angie shivered or so he thought. He glanced down and realized she was laughing and trying to keep her two cousins from catching her at it. She buried her face against his chest.

Justin and Harlan whirled to take off, but Clint released Angela with some reluctance and placed himself squarely in their path, one hand firmly on each boy's shoulder. He regarded them steadily. "Now here's the deal, guys. You keep very, very quiet about what you saw and I will keep my mouth shut about the cigarettes you were sneaking."

Despite being plenty old enough to smoke the two teens exchanged guilty looks. They knew how vehemently their grandfather objected. Harlan had gone on about it earlier.

"Are we agreed?" Clint asked.

"Oh, yeah," Justin said fervently. "Even at my age Dad would knock me from here to Dallas if he knew I was smoking."

"From here to Kansas," Harlan concurred. "We never saw a thing, Mr. Brady." He dared a glance at his cousin. "Sorry, Angie. We didn't mean to interrupt."

"Yeah," Justin said. "You guys go back to doing whatever it was you were doing when we showed up. Not that we noticed or anything."

"Later, guys," Clint said. "And ditch the cigarettes."

They took off running. Away from the house, Clint noticed with amusement.

"How'd you know they'd been smoking?" Angie asked when they were out of earshot. "I never smelled a thing."

"Guesswork," he admitted. "They looked guilty as sin when your grandfather was talking about cigarettes. My brothers and I used to sneak out and try to catch a smoke after some family gathering, so we could feel grown-up. It was my mother who caught up with us the second or third time we tried it. She was not pleased. She threatened to shred the tobacco like a salad and make us eat it for dessert, if she ever caught us with a cigarette again. She said if we were going to put that foul stuff into our bodies, we might as well chow down on it. Said it would kill us quicker that way."

"Did she do it?"

"Never had to. We'd gotten the message."

She studied him, her expression thoughtful. "You never talked much about your family when we were together," she said.

"Neither did you," he pointed out.

"*Touché*. Maybe we should start all over again, pretend we just met."

He glanced at her protruding belly. "That's a little hard to do, don't you think?"

Suddenly she gasped and grabbed her stomach.

"What?" he demanded at once. "Are you okay? Sweet heaven, you're not going into labor, are you? It's too soon, isn't it? Have you even seen a doctor since you got here?"

"Whoa. Relax." She grinned. "Your kid was just making his presence felt. I think he's practicing for the NFL already."

"You're convinced it's a boy?"

"No, but Consuela is. She's almost never wrong." She regarded him shyly, then took his hand and placed it on her stomach. "Here, feel."

For several seconds he felt nothing at all, then suddenly he felt the *thump* of a very solid kick. The rush of feelings that came over him was mind-boggling. For the first time, the baby was a reality, not just part of some grand lie that stood between them.

"A field goal kicker, for sure," he said, feeling the unexpected sting of tears in his eyes.

He'd missed months of this. He'd been cheated of hearing his baby's heartbeat for the first time, of seeing Angela's body change to accommodate the child she was carrying. OK, so that was partly his fault, but she was the one who'd impetuously taken off. She was the one who'd kept on running.

"Damn you," he said softly.

She stared at him in shock. Her eyes filled with hurt and confusion at the harshness of his words. "What?"

"You've robbed me of so much."

Never one to take an accusation lightly, she scowled back at him. Temper flared in her eyes. "You had a choice," she reminded him stiffly. "You could have reacted like a man and accepted responsibility from the beginning."

It was the same old story, dragging them back to square one. Clint sighed. If he were entirely honest, he'd have to admit they shared the blame. There was more than enough to go around. Even so, he couldn't resist one last dig.

"Is that all you expected, for me to accept responsibility? I never questioned that this was my baby. Not once. I was always under the impression what you really wanted was for me to declare my love and marry you."

"It's the same thing," she said defiantly.

"Not quite, angel. And if you were being entirely honest, you'd admit that back then you and I were nowhere close to sorting out our feelings for each other. You didn't even trust me enough to tell me the truth about who you were."

Her lips compressed into an angry line before she snapped, "Don't talk to me about honesty, Clint Brady. You've never once owned up to what you're really doing here."

He went absolutely still at the unspoken accusation behind the words. "Meaning?"

"Just how did you find out who I was and where to find me? Was finding out that I came from a wealthy family enough to drag you down here after me?"

She had hinted at as much earlier, but Clint still

couldn't believe his ears. The unfairness of her charge apparently never crossed her mind. Quick-tempered retorts came into his head, but he knew if he spoke even one of them, ugly words would start flying fast and furiously. Their tempers had always been their downfall. There was no such thing as a quiet, rational conversation between Hattie and him over even a small difference of opinion. They shouted whatever came to mind at full volume.

When the dust settled, there were always hurt feelings and fences to mend. He suspected it was the one area in life that didn't improve with practice. He suspected the cuts just went deeper and the fences grew harder and harder to mend. Maybe it was time to break the cycle and find a new way of getting along. Since he didn't have an imagination vivid enough to figure out how to do that on the spur of the moment, he decided some distance was called for.

"Go back inside, Angela," he said abruptly, backing away from her. "It's too damned cold for you to be out here."

"I will not," she said, digging in her heels literally and regarding him with fire in her eyes. "You don't make decisions for me."

"Oh, for pity's sake, can't you do one thing because it's sensible and stop worrying about the fact that the suggestion came out of my mouth?"

With that he scooped her up in his arms and headed for the house. After a moment of stunned silence, she blistered the air with protests loud enough to wake the dead. Half the family was standing in the kitchen watching by the time he deposited her unceremoniously on her feet inside the door. Thank heaven no one laughed or she probably would have grabbed the carving knife lying in plain sight by the turkey and come after them.

He turned on his heel, then, and struck off for a very long walk. He glanced at the sky, hoping for signs of an impending blizzard. He'd figured no less than a foot of snow was likely to cool his temper anytime tonight.

He'd been walking for the better part of an hour, his face chilled, his hands jammed into his pockets, the wind cutting through his coat, when he saw Luke Adams walking slowly in his direction. He had the feeling Angela's father would either go or stay at a signal from him. He gave the older man a curt nod that was apparently accepted as welcome enough.

"I suppose you'll be wanting me to leave now," he said eventually.

He thought he caught a glimpse of Luke's smile in the moonlight.

"Not unless you want to," Angela's father said. "You're going to have to make up your own mind what the best solution is to this. You and Angela. If you decide to stay, we'll welcome you. If you decide to go, we'll look out for Angela and the baby."

"And hate my guts for the rest of your days," Clint concluded.

"Hating is a waste of time and energy," Luke said.

He said it with such passionate conviction that Clint stared at him. "You ever hated anyone?"

"Myself for a long time," Luke said candidly. "My father for a bit."

The response stunned Clint. If Luke could hate a man like Harlan Adams, then there was no word for the depth of his own feelings toward his father. "You hated your father? How'd that happen?"

Deeply felt sorrow seemed to etch new lines in Luke's rugged face. "I figured between us we killed my brother," he explained, echoing the story that Angela had told Clint earlier. "I also resented the hell out of the fact that he was trying to control my life. Jessie was the one who made me see that the only thing in life that really counts is family. When you love people, you work out your differences, no matter how difficult it is or how long it takes. I was never a big talker, so it was always harder for me."

"I know what you mean," Clint said. "I always figured actions ought to speak loudly enough."

"I'd say yours do," Luke said with a grin. "They were loud and clear earlier tonight."

"Sorry," Clint apologized again. "That woman can make me angry quicker than you can set off a rocket on the Fourth of July."

"So I noticed, but that wasn't what fascinated me so."

"Oh?"

"What I saw was a man who cared enough about a woman to make sure she was in out of the cold, even when he was mad enough to throttle her. That's the kind of man I could respect." He gave Clint a direct look. "It's something to think about, isn't it?"

Before Clint could respond, Luke headed for the

barn and left him with nothing but his thoughts for company.

At least there was one member of the Adams clan that didn't think he was here with an ulterior motive, he concluded bitterly. Too bad it wasn't Angela.

Where she'd gotten the nut-brained idea that he was after the Adams fortune was beyond him. He hadn't even known she had a dime to her name when he'd traced her to Dallas and met Betsy. If he was an ambitious, money-hungry kind of man, would he have been scrambling to make ends meet on a broken-down ranch in Montana? There were far easier ways to make a buck.

He just happened to love ranching. He liked the exhausting work and the never-ending challenges and the intellectual stimulation of figuring out how to better his herd from year to year. It might never make him rich, but fulfillment was all he was after. It was enough to have something of his own, something he could take pride in. If Angela hadn't seen that much in their months together, then she hadn't really known him at all. And it was damned sure he hadn't known her.

"Well, that was certainly humiliating," Angela said, when she'd finally calmed down enough to speak. Most of the family had discreetly slipped away, leaving her in the kitchen with two of her cousins and Consuela.

"I thought it was romantic," Sharon Lynn said with huge eyes and an exaggerated sigh.

Sharon Lynn was less than a year younger than

Angela, but she'd stayed in Los Pinos her whole life, surrounded by family, content with running Eli Dolan's Drugstore, where her mother had once worked and where her mother and Cody had carried on much of their highly irregular and high-volume courtship. Maybe that explained why she thought that Clint's he-man act was so romantic. She wasn't worldly enough or liberated enough to know better.

"You want him, you can have him," Angela snapped.

Her cousin laughed. "Not on your life. I'm not wasting my energy chasing after a man who's already hooked."

"Besides, she already has eyes for Kyle Mason," Dani said. She gave Angela a sympathetic look. "Are you okay?"

"Just peachy."

Dani, who was now a veterinarian in town, urged Angie toward the kitchen table. "Sit down. Your hands are like ice." She glanced around the kitchen until her gaze found Consuela. "Could you make her some tea, please?"

Angela accepted the tea and the solicitude. Dani hadn't been born an Adams. She'd been adopted by Jordan when he and her mother, Kelly Flint, had married. She was older than Angela by four years, but it seemed to Angela that something had changed in her cousin.

Angela studied her intently, trying to figure out what it was exactly. Once exuberant and outgoing, Dani now seemed shy and quiet, even as she managed to take charge of the situation. Obviously her veterinary training had enabled her to cope well with unexpected emergencies, but there was a vulnerability about her that was out of character.

When she handed the cup of tea to Angela, her worried gaze shifted away the instant Angela made eye contact with her. Angela put the cup on the table and caught her cousin's hand. "You OK?"

Dani's responding smile seemed forced. "Hey, you're the patient, not me."

"It must be nice having a patient who can tell you what's wrong for a change," she teased. "I'm just cold. It'll pass." She sobered and added quietly, "There's something else going on with you."

"Don't be silly. I'm perfectly fine."

Sharon Lynn stepped in and circled an arm protectively around Dani's waist. She met Angela's gaze evenly. "Let it go," she said quietly, but firmly.

Angela was taken aback by the fierce joining of forces. The cousins had all been close growing up. There'd been no way around it, with family gatherings as common as Texas bluebonnets in summer. They'd never taken sides back then. In fact, the girls had all been amazingly compatible, practically as close as sisters. Had things changed since she'd been gone? Was she now viewed as an outsider? Were there secrets that would never be shared with her?

"I'm sorry if I pushed," she apologized.

Dani gave her hand a quick squeeze. "Don't worry about it." Her expression turned briskly professional and her gaze warmed. "How are you feeling now? Better?"

"I'm warmer," she said.

"But still unsettled," Dani guessed. "Clint strikes me as the kind of man who could keep a woman unsettled."

"He is a royal pain in the—"

"Whoops," Sharon Lynn said with a laugh. "Don't get her started again. There won't be enough chamomile tea on earth to calm her down."

"Maybe you should go upstairs and rest," Dani said.

"No," Angela protested.

"A few more weeks and you'll be begging for rest," Dani warned.

"Not with me around," Consuela said. "I cannot wait to hold this child in my arms. Angela will have to fight me for a chance to take care of the little one."

"You're still spoiled rotten, I see," Sharon Lynn said to Angela, even as she reached up and squeezed Consuela's hand. She eyed her cousin speculatively. "Have you ever actually held a job?"

"Don't be mean," Dani said.

The familiar bickering made Angela smile, even though she was the butt of the teasing. "Actually, I've held quite a few jobs."

"Couldn't keep one, huh?" Sharon Lynn taunted.

"You just wait until this baby is born. I'll take over the soda fountain for you one day and my milk shakes will have the residents of Los Pinos weeping."

"Have you ever actually worked a soda fountain?" Dani inquired skeptically.

"No, but I worked a bar. How different can it be?"

"My customers are sober," Sharon Lynn pointed out. "They know what they're getting."

Angela grinned at her. "Oh, how I've missed you two. Nobody could ever put me in my place the way you do."

"Not even Clint?" Sharon Lynn asked.

The back door slammed open just then, caught by the wind as Clint tried to enter. "Not even Clint what?" he asked, his gaze fixed on her.

"Not a thing," Sharon Lynn said.

"See you," Dani said, dragging her cousin out of the room.

Consuela snatched up a silver coffee service and slipped out behind them.

"Et tu, Brute?" Angela muttered.

"I do not know this Brute," Consuela said, then leaned down to whisper, "Talk to the man, *niña*. Do not stop talking until you have reached an understanding. *¿Si?"*

Angela glanced up into Clint's stormy eyes and shuddered. She had the distinct impression that quiet conversation was the last thing on his mind.

Chapter Eight

"Are you planning to apologize?" Angela asked Clint, figuring that a preemptive strike was called for.

"Me? You were the one throwing insults around," Clint shot right back, his blue eyes as stormy as a hurricane-tossed sea.

"Maybe we should take turns," she suggested cheerfully. "I'll apologize for making disparaging insinuations about your character, and you can apologize for being a dyed-in-the-wool macho jerk."

His gaze narrowed at the deliberate insult. "You're not off to a very promising start with that apology."

"Sorry." She smiled. "Best I can do."

"Let me get this straight. Are you admitting that you know perfectly well that I'm not after the family fortune?"

She thought about that for a minute. It was apparently about fifty-nine seconds too long, judging by the increasingly furious expression on his face. His righteous indignation did carry some weight with her. He'd never been an especially good actor. His emotions were always right out there in plain view. If he'd ever lied to her, she was pretty sure she would have known it. Of course, he'd probably thought the same of her. Maybe both of them were just plain lousy at character assessment.

"OK, I admit it," she said eventually.

He regarded her skeptically. "Say it like you mean it, angel."

"I know you didn't come here because of my family's money," she said solemnly.

"Mind telling me who sowed that idea in your head in the first place?"

Now that was tricky turf. She didn't want him to realize that her grandfather had been speculating about his honesty. They seemed to have built a good rapport in a very short time. She didn't want to force Clint's pride to kick in. It would destroy that relationship before it ever got a decent chance.

She bit back a sigh. No matter how she fibbed to herself about wanting Clint to back off and leave, the truth was she liked having him here, liked seeing him slowly becoming a part of the family. Getting along with Grandpa Harlan was a huge part of that. Perhaps her grandfather had had his doubts about Clint, but she wanted to believe Clint could prove to him there had been no merit to those doubts.

"It was just the only thing I could come up with

to explain your persistence," she told him, skirting the truth by a wide margin.

He studied her intently for some time, then shook his head. "I never thought I'd say this, especially given recent evidence to the contrary, but you're a terrible liar, angel. If you came up with that notion all on your own, then I'm Billy the Kid."

The irony of the remark wasn't lost on her. "I guess I used to be more convincing, huh?"

"Much more convincing," he agreed. "So, 'fess up. Who was it?"

She debated lying again, then decided there wasn't any point to it. He was the kind of man who'd nag at it and sooner or later, he'd figure out the truth. Maybe it would be better if she told him. She settled for an explanation that was true as far as it went and left her grandfather out of it.

"Janet, actually."

"Janet," he repeated, his expression more thoughtful than furious. "I should have known. Was she advising you to protect yourself from my greedy clutches?"

"Something like that."

"She was just thinking like an attorney, I suppose."

"Exactly."

His gaze clashed with hers. "Unless your grandfather was the one who put the idea into *her* head. Was he?"

"Does it really matter?" Angela asked hurriedly. "The bottom line is Janet was looking out for my best interests the way any good attorney would."

"Did she want you to insist on a prenuptial agreement?"

"As a matter of fact, yes."

"Not a bad idea," he said calmly enough, though his eyes were once again turbulent. "Did you agree?"

"We're not getting married so what's the point?" she retorted.

"Let's just say we were, would you want the agreement?"

"Yes," she said instinctively, then hastily retracted it. "No. Dammit, Clint, I don't know what makes sense."

"You really don't trust me, do you?" he asked, sounding more defeated than angry.

"Do you trust me?" she shot back.

His grin was rueful. "Maybe not, but there's one big difference, darlin'. I've never betrayed you the way you betrayed me. I may have been a fool back in Montana, I may not have responded to your announcement the way you'd been expecting, but I have never betrayed you or lied to you. I accepted you at face value. Apparently you can't say the same."

She swallowed hard against the tide of hurt that washed over her at his charge. She couldn't deny it, either. He was right. He had far more reason to distrust her than she did him.

"Where does that leave us?" she asked, suddenly exhausted by the tension of the past few hours.

He leveled a look straight into her eyes, a look

filled with questions and regrets. Then he sighed. "I wish to hell I knew, angel. I wish I knew."

Clint left the kitchen feeling more hopeless than he ever had in his life. To her everlasting credit, his mother had raised a houseful of optimists. She had refused to blame his father for walking out on them. She had never said a harsh word about the man who had left her to cope with all those children and a mountain of debts. She had just taken his departure as one more challenge to make them all stronger.

All of them had grown up believing that with just a little effort life could be better than it had been. He wouldn't say his brothers and sisters were over-achievers, but they were undaunted by a good challenge. They'd heard the old adage about turning life's lemons into lemonade so often, none of them could drink the stuff.

He'd been the same until today. He'd been fortunate enough to go a lifetime without being distrusted. Back home, folks knew the Bradys were honest, if poor. In Montana, he'd paid off every debt he owed, including the ranch. As of last month, it was his free and clear. If he gave his word, he kept it. No one had ever had cause to worry about the kind of man he was.

Now these people who didn't know him at all found his motives suspect. He supposed it was natural enough that they would worry about one of their own, that they would think first of protecting Angela, but the instinctive lack of trust in him cut just the same. Worse, he had no idea how to rectify it. Words weren't the answer. And actions, the kind of actions that would deepen respect and engender real trust, took time, time he didn't have.

Sooner or later he would have to head back to Montana. He had a good foreman there looking after things now, but he couldn't rely on Hardy Jenkins shouldering the burden of running the ranch forever.

As he trudged up the stairs, it seemed he carried the weight of the world. Maybe he'd feel better with a good night's sleep. Maybe in the morning he'd have the answers that eluded him tonight.

He was halfway to his room—it was a damn suite, actually—when the man most on his mind exited a room down the hall. Harlan Adams smiled, his expression totally open and free of guile. Maybe he was already overcoming his suspicions, Clint thought hopefully.

"You aren't sneaking off to bed at this hour, are you?" Harlan asked.

"I was considering it," Clint admitted. "I've got some thinking to do."

"Not when there's a poker game about to start downstairs in Luke's office," he insisted. "Son, that would be downright foolish. Nothing takes a man's mind off his troubles better than a game of cards. You haven't played poker until you've played with us. Before the night's out, one of us is bound to bet the whole damn ranch."

"With my luck, I'd win it," Clint muttered under his breath. That would really win the family over, he thought.

"Never can tell, you might," Harlan said, proving

his hearing was as sharp as ever. He looped a powerful arm around Clint's shoulders and propelled him back downstairs.

"Almost lost my own spread to Janet once," he confided. "That woman can play poker. She's got a sneaky side to her nature. Jenny's the same way. They even won over old Mule, God rest his soul."

"Mule?"

Harlan grinned. "Cantankerous man, but the best danged card player in Los Pinos. Mule had vowed never to play cards with a woman, but those two changed his mind. He said the kind of gumption and daring they had with a lousy pair of deuces was downright scary."

"Will they be playing tonight?" Clint asked, trying to imagine the fierce competitiveness of husband against wife and daughter. From what he'd observed of Janet and Jenny, it ought to be amusing.

"Hell, no," Harlan declared fervently. "I can't have the two of them showing me up in front of my own boys, can I? Besides if Jenny ever gets her hands on another share of White Pines, she's threatened to put a Bloomingdales on it. I can't have that, even if she does swear that without a few fancy department stores around she'll move back east one day, just so she can spend a decent day shopping."

"And you believe her?"

"Did once," he claimed. "I'm not so sure anymore. Not since she's discovered Nieman-Marcus. Of course, with Jenny you never know quite what to expect. She's a lot like her mama that way, lively and unpredictable."

To Clint's amusement, he actually sounded as if he considered it possible that one day Jenny would impulsively erect a huge store on his property just so she could shop. It also seemed as if it didn't bother him all that much. Before Clint could analyze how a man could be so blasé about losing his land, they reached Luke's office.

"Look who I've roped into joining us," Harlan announced as they entered.

"Ah, another lamb to the slaughter," Cody retorted. "Do you have any card sense at all?"

"I've played a game or two," Clint said.

"Which probably means he won half of Montana playing poker," Jordan assessed.

"It was blackjack, actually," Clint said, only partially in jest. He hadn't won his land that night, but he'd won the down payment for it.

"Does everybody have their deeds tucked away in a vault back home?" Luke inquired dryly as he poured Clint a shot of whiskey and set it in front of him.

"Are you kidding? Kelly won't even tell me where she has ours for safekeeping," Jordan replied.

"Melissa either," Cody added.

"Janet and I don't have secrets," Harlan boasted. "I know precisely where the deeds are."

"Sure you do," Luke taunted. "In her office, locked in *her* vault."

"Okay, okay, enough of this nonsense," Harlan grumbled. "Who's dealing?"

"We'll cut for it. High card deals," Luke said, shuffling the deck one last time.

Clint pulled a ten and figured that was the end of it. He waited for one of the others to come up with an ace or even a jack. Instead, the ten took it and Luke handed him the cards, along with a warning.

"We take this seriously, son. No fancy games and nothing wild."

"Except our manners," Cody said. "As the night wears on, we forget everything our mama taught us."

"We get drunk," Harlan translated. "One of us tries to stay sober enough to haul the others up to bed."

"Who's turn is it?" Cody asked.

"Yours," Luke and Jordan taunted, removing the tumbler of whiskey in front of him.

"I think Clint ought to do it," Cody protested.

"And have him see us at our worst and remember it? No way," Harlan said. "We might end up with our faces on the front page of the Dallas papers."

Clint stiffened at the suggestion that he'd resort to blackmail. It was only part of the rowdy teasing he was sure went on all the time with these men, but it cut a little too close to the accusations he'd all too recently been discussing with Angela. Thievery, blackmail, what would be next?

He glanced across the table and saw that Harlan was observing him with a steady gaze. He thought there was a message in that gaze, but he was damned if he could read it.

"Five-card draw," he said quietly and dealt the cards.

Luke won the first hand, which had the rest of them accusing Clint of stacking the deck to win over his prospective father-in-law. When Luke won the second hand as well, a hand dealt by Jordan, the men went silent.

They played now with a fierce intensity, the same way they did everything else. They'd played for a couple of hours when the cards began falling Clint's way. The chips stacked up in front of him. He had a nice bundle, when Harlan glanced at his watch and declared the evening over.

"That's it, boys. It's after midnight and I'm getting too old for this nonsense."

"Janet got you on a limited budget?" Luke teased.

"Nope, I just know when a man's on a roll. If the rest of you can't see it, then stay here and lose a few more dollars. I'm going up to my nice, warm bed and my nice, warm wife."

"Ah," Luke said. "Now that's a concept I can embrace." He, too, stood up.

"I guess that's it, then," Jordan said. "Congratulations, Clint. Nice playing. I think I hear Kelly calling me, too."

"Melissa's been calling to me for the past hour, but you haven't seen me dashing off to bed," Cody protested. "Besides, you guys, what about poor Clint? He doesn't have a wife upstairs."

"He can rectify that anytime he wants to," Luke responded dryly.

"I wonder about that," Clint said sorrowfully. "Angela doesn't seem inclined to make an honest man of me."

"Are you asking for our advice?" Harlan asked

eagerly, clearly ready to sit down again if called upon for some wisdom about the battle of the sexes.

Clint laughed at the four men who were poised to stay and help him out with courting Angela. "Thanks, anyway," he said. "I have the feeling you all would just get me in more trouble than I'm in already."

"You're probably right," Cody said. "Not a one of us can claim our courtships were smooth sailing."

"And none of us learned a darned thing from our mistakes," Jordan added. "You go with your own instincts, Clint. You're the one she's in love with. Even I can see the way she looks at you and Kelly claims I'm clueless on emotional issues. You must have been doing something right up there in Montana."

After they'd gone, as Clint made his way upstairs, he tried to remember exactly what he'd done to impress Hattie Jones. About the only thing he recalled with any certainty was seducing her on the night they'd met. It wasn't a tactic he could try with the woman eight and a half months pregnant.

Or was it? He paused at the top of the steps and stared at the closed door opposite his own. Was Angela lying in bed wide awake, tormented by thoughts of lovemaking the way he'd been night after night? What would she do if he slipped quietly into her room and settled himself into bed beside her, if only to hold her close until morning? How long would it take her to wake the household? He envisioned a whole line of very shaky guns aimed in his direction. Drunk as they all were when they'd parted, at least one of them was still bound to hit him if they accidentally fired.

Even with that image sharply defined in his head, he reached for the doorknob and quietly turned it. He stepped into the room and closed the door behind him, then waited, his heart thundering in his chest, to see if his movements had disturbed her.

"You might's well come all the way in," she said as if she'd been wide awake and expecting him. "What's the matter? Did you lose your way back to your own room?"

His eyes adjusted to the room's darkness and his gaze sought out the bed. Though the covers were tangled, there was no sign of Angela in it. Besides, even through his alcohol-induced haze, he grasped the fact that the bed was on his left and her voice had come from somewhere on his right.

"Angel?"

"Yes," she said, her amusement plain. "I'm over here, by the window."

He saw her then, seated in a rocking chair beside the huge bay window. A faint trail of moonlight shimmered over her. She had brushed her hair out of its usual careless knot so that it fell in glorious waves to her shoulders. Against the creaminess of her skin and the stark white of her nightgown, her hair shimmered like a cascade of garnets, dark red and mysterious and sensual. Quite simply, she took his breath away.

"You truly do look like an angel," he whispered, awestruck as always by her beauty.

"And you look like a man who's spent the eve-

PLAY "LUCKY 7" AND GET
FIVE FREE GIFTS!

HOW TO PLAY:

1. With a coin, carefully scratch off the silver box at the right. Then check the claim chart to see what we have for you—**FREE BOOKS** and a gift—**ALL YOURS! ALL FREE!**

2. Send back this card and you'll receive brand-new Silhouette Special Edition® novels. These books have a cover price of $3.99 each, but they are yours to keep absolutely free.

3. There's no catch. You're under no obligation to buy anything. We charge nothing—  ZERO—for your first shipment. And you don't have to make any minimum number of purchases—not even one!

4. The fact is thousands of readers enjoy receiving books by mail from the Silhouette Reader Service™ months before they're available in stores. They like the convenience of home delivery and they love our discount prices!

5. We hope that after receiving your free books you'll want to remain a subscriber. But the choice is yours—to continue or cancel, any time at all! So why not take us up on our invitation, with no risk of any kind. You'll be glad you did!

YOURS FREE!

This lovely necklace will add glamour to your most elegant outfit! Its cobra-link chain is a generous 18" long, and its lustrous simulated cultured pearl is mounted in an attractive pendant! Best of all, it's ABSOLUTELY FREE, just for accepting our NO-RISK offer.

NOT ACTUAL SIZE

ning in a saloon," she retorted dryly. "You're weaving a bit, cowboy. Sit down before you fall down. Did you have a good time with the Adams card sharks?"

"I did, indeed. I won."

He thought her eyes widened a bit in surprise at that.

"Really?"

He pulled his winnings from his pockets and allowed the bills to flutter into her lap. There was a satisfying heap of them when he was done.

"My, my," she said, fingering a fifty. "Must have been pretty high stakes."

"High enough," he agreed. "But nobody bet their ranch."

"You sound disappointed."

He regarded her sadly. "Not that again, angel. I don't want your money. I don't want your land. How many times do I have to say it before you believe me?"

She regarded him speculatively. "What do you want, then?"

"You," he said without hesitation. "Just you."

Moonlight caught the sheen of tears in her eyes. The sight of them distressed him. "Are you crying?" he asked, kneeling in front of her. He brushed the dampness from her face. "Don't cry, darlin'. Please don't cry."

"It's okay. I just wish..." Her voice trailed off.

"You wish what?"

She reached toward him and her fingers sifted

through his hair, then came to rest on his cheek. "I just wish you meant it."

"I do mean it," he insisted. "From the night we met, I've wanted you. There's never been another woman like you. You make me..."

"Crazy?" she supplied.

"Angel, angel," he protested, "where's your sense of romance?"

"Sleeping," she said briskly. "That's what we ought to be doing, too. Everyone will be heading out at the crack of dawn. And tomorrow we start all over again at White Pines."

Clint stilled. He hadn't considered the possibility that everyone might go off somewhere for Christmas. Where would that leave him? Was he expected to head on home? Maybe linger back here alone? Or were they automatically assuming he'd be coming along?

He wondered if he could convince Angela to stay right here with him. They could have their own private holiday celebration, maybe even sort out where they were going without all the well-meaning interference. He was about to suggest just that when he realized that she was describing the last Christmas she'd spent with the whole family.

"It was just like today, only better. There were tons of presents, because everybody has always gone overboard. Consuela and her cousin Maritza, who works for Grandpa Harlan, fixed enough food to last for a month. Grandpa waited to put up his tree until we all got there, so we could decorate it together. We sang carols while we did it, then we all traipsed off to midnight services.'' She sighed. ''It was wonderful. Year after year we had the exact same tradition.''

''And you've missed it, haven't you?''

''More than anything else we do,'' she admitted. Her gaze caught his. ''Will you come with us? Will you share it with me this year?''

The invitation pleased him more than he cared to admit. ''If that's what you want.''

''It is.''

''Someday soon, though, you and I are going to have to sit down and talk, all by ourselves, without any interruptions or distractions. The baby's going to be here any day now and we have to get things settled.''

''No,'' she said sharply.

He stared at her. ''What do you mean, no?''

''I will not make any sort of a decision about anything just because we have a deadline staring us in the face. Whatever happens between us, whatever conclusions we reach about the future will be made when the time is right and not a minute before that.''

Clint stared at her in frustration. ''Dammit, I want this baby to be born with my name.''

''That's what I wanted seven months ago, and you were in no big hurry to accommodate me.''

He stood up and began to pace. ''So this is payback? You're going to punish the baby, make the kid start life without his father's name, just because you want to get even with me? How can you be so cruel and heartless?''

''Of course that's not what I want,'' she snapped.

"But I will not marry you just so the baby can have your name. I'll put your name on the birth certificate. You'll have your claim to paternity, but any relationship between you and me is going to have to be based on something else, something just between the two of us." Her flashing eyes clashed with his. "Is that clear enough?" she demanded.

"Oh, it's crystal clear," he muttered as he headed for the door. He paused to take one last shot. "Since you have Janet covering all your legal angles, maybe it's about time I found an attorney of my own."

He heard her sharply indrawn breath across the room. Good, he'd struck a nerve.

"Clint, no," she protested, sounding panicked by his impulsive threat.

He refused to back down. Meeting her gaze evenly, he said, "Good night, angel. Sweet dreams."

He closed the door softly behind him, even though he would have preferred to slam it shut. That would have awakened the whole household, though, and he was in no mood to explain the latest argument he and Angela had had.

It seemed lately as if every time they tried to talk, it disintegrated into some sort of name-calling argument. Hadn't he concluded not more than a half hour earlier that it was time for actions, not word? There was no time like the present to get started, with his ire roused and his inhibitions weakened by whiskey.

He threw open the door and crossed the room in three angry strides. She had risen from the rocking chair and stood halfway between it and the bed, her gaze startled. Without a word, he pulled her into his arms and delivered a kiss meant to take her breath away.

She gave a soft yelp of surprise, then a soft sigh of pleasure as he peppered kisses across her face. He found the hem of her gown and lifted it, his fingers sliding over silky flesh that had filled out into lush, provocative curves.

When he reached her belly, he slowed and the nature of his touch changed to one of awe. Her skin was stretched taut, and beneath the surface, he felt the stirring of his child. His mood altered in a heartbeat. All of the anger dissolved. Lust gave way to something tender.

With a sigh that was part dismay, part frustration, he rested his forehead against hers.

"I'm sorry," he said, his breathing ragged.

"No, I am."

"We can't go on like this, fighting until our nerves are raw. We'll end up saying something one of these days that we can't take back."

"I know."

"Maybe we should put some distance between us, think about this," he suggested.

"Not again," she said.

The fierceness of her reaction startled him. "No?"

"Absolutely not. You're not running and neither am I. We will settle this, Clint. Let's just take one day at a time. Let's enjoy Christmas and maybe the rest will take care of itself." She rested her hand against his cheek, then smiled. "After all, it is the season of miracles."

Chapter Nine

Angela wasn't sure what had possessed her to invite Clint along to White Pines. She was asking for trouble, no doubt about it. Maybe she'd been persuaded because she didn't think she could shake him any easier than a horse could rid itself of a burr under its saddle. Maybe it was simple politeness.

More than likely, though, it had something to do with sentiment. They had spent the previous Christmas together, and despite all her reminiscing the night before about past holidays with her family, Christmas with Clint in Montana had been one of the most incredible of her entire life. She smiled to herself just thinking about it.

They had gone out the day before Christmas, tromped through a foot or more of hard-packed snow until they'd found the perfect tree. Clint had chopped it down and hauled it back to the ranch, grumbling all the way about the size of it. He'd sounded exactly the way her father did every year, which had made her homesick. In some peculiar way, it had also reassured her. Seeing similarities in the two men she cared most about suggested that her judgment wasn't all bad.

Since an earlier search of the house had turned up not one single strand of lights or an ornament, Angela had gone into town after the tree was up and gathered everything she could think of to decorate the ceiling-scraping monster of a pine. Clint had taken one look at the bags of cranberries, packages of popcorn and yards of ribbon and shaken his head.

"I don't know, darlin'," he'd said, his expression doubtful. "This is looking an awful lot like work."

"You just wait," she'd promised. "We are going to have the most spectacular, old-fashioned Christmas tree you've ever seen. Start popping the corn, okay? I'll get busy with the cranberries."

They had sipped hot chocolate and played carols on the stereo as they'd worked. They'd eaten as much popcorn as they'd strung, but by evening the tree was crisscrossed with strands of white and red. Colorful red and green bows added a festive touch. Clint had flat-out balked when she'd wanted to add candles in place of lights.

"Enough's enough," he'd declared. "I don't want the ranch to burn down in the name of having some Christmas decorations straight out of 'Little House on the Prairie.' I'll go get lights, if you insist on having them."

"The store's sold out," she said, disappointed by his reaction.

He'd leaned down and kissed her. "Trust me, Hattie. I never make a promise if I don't think I can deliver."

She had started cooking while he was gone, sure that this was one promise he wouldn't be able to keep. She'd consoled herself by making every dish she remembered from Christmas dinners back home: turkey with corn bread stuffing, cranberry relish, mashed potatoes, gravy and two gigantic pumpkin pies.

It was dark by the time Clint had gotten home and the house was filled with the familiar scents of pine and cinnamon and roasting turkey. He'd stood in the doorway, shaking the snow from his coat, and sniffed appreciatively.

"It smells like Christmas in here."

She had grinned. "It's true what they say, the sense of smell does bring back memories, doesn't it?" She eyed the bag in his hand speculatively. "Lights?"

He'd tossed it to her. "Enough to rival some big-city skyscraper at night," he declared.

Eagerly she had opened the bag and found a half-dozen strands of tiny white lights, six hundred in all. Her mother would have been in raptures.

"Oh, this is going to be wonderful," she'd said, already imagining it. "I can't wait to see it."

Putting the lights on after the fact had been tedious and at times hilarious as they'd gotten tangled up in popcorn and cranberries, but the results had been worth it. The tree simply glowed, sparkling like a night sky with a million stars.

"You really get into this Christmas stuff, don't you?" Clint asked, watching her.

"Sure. Don't you?"

He'd shrugged indifferently. She'd tried to question him about his own holiday memories, but he'd cut the conversation short and won her silence by saying that the memories they made together were the only ones that mattered to him now. The sweet remark had brought tears to her eyes.

Clint had reached in his pocket then and handed her a small, gaily wrapped package.

Surprised, Angela had stared at it. "What's this?"

Clint grinned sheepishly. "What does it look like?"

"A Christmas present? For me?"

"It is Christmas, isn't it?"

"Yes, but—"

"You thought I'd forgotten."

"Something like that."

"Aren't you going to open it? Or would you rather wait until morning?"

"No, no, now is fine." She hadn't been sure she would be able to stand the suspense until morning.

Her fingers fumbled with the ribbon, which had been so artfully tied it was evident that a store clerk, not Clint, had been responsible for it. "It's beautiful."

"If you're that impressed with the wrapping, I can't wait to see your expression once you get it open," he'd said dryly.

"At this rate I may never get it open. My hands are shaking."

He'd reached out and clasped them between his, stilling her efforts. "Hattie, it's not a big deal. It's just a present, a token really."

Eyes tearing, she had gazed at him. "It's a big deal to me. It's the first present you've ever given me."

"Are you worried about my taste?"

"No, absolutely not. Anything you picked out will be special to me."

He'd let her finish unwrapping it then. The flat velvet box made her heart thump unsteadily and once again she was all thumbs as she tried to lift the lid. Inside, against a white satin pillow, rested a gold pendant, a tiny Christmas tree with winking jewels as decorations. A diamond sparkled at the top.

"I thought maybe it would remind you of our first Christmas together," he'd said, looking awkward and uncomfortable at the sentimental gesture.

"Nothing you could have gotten me would have meant more," she swore to him. "Nothing." Eyes shimmering with unshed tears, she gazed at him. "Help me put it on."

It was his turn to fumble as he tried to manage the small clasp. When the necklace was secure, she gazed at herself in the mirror. The emerald, ruby and sapphire chips twinkled gaily against the soft gleam of gold as the pendant rested against her bright green sweater. He stood behind her in front of an oval mirror, his hands on her shoulders, as she'd admired the necklace. Lifting her gaze, her reflected glance caught his.

"Merry Christmas, darlin'," he'd whispered.

"Merry Christmas."

Now, thinking of that moment and the love she had been so sure she had seen shining in his eyes, she reached up and touched the pendant resting against her skin. She had worn it ever since, no matter the season, because it had reminded her of the man she had fallen in love with one lonely winter in Montana.

Could they recapture what they had felt that night? Or could they only move on to create new memories? When the new year began, would they still be together or would they have resolved to go their own separate ways, connected only by the child they had conceived together?

Her baby stirred restlessly in her womb as if he, too, was anxious to know the answers to those questions.

"I want us to be a family," she murmured, admitting it for the first time in a very long time.

Whether that was possible, though, was up to Clint. If he couldn't love her after what she'd done, if he couldn't forgive her for pretending to be the mythical Hattie Jones, then she would have to let him go.

"And we'll be just fine," she promised her child.

The baby kicked in apparent protest.

"We will," she repeated fiercely, her hands on her belly. "But I won't give up without a fight, little one. I promise you that, too."

* * *

This was the first Clint had actually seen of the town of Los Pinos. It was miles beyond Luke's ranch and beyond the home where he'd spent the night with Betsy's family. Gazing at the quaint, unpretentious stores and homey restaurants, he felt immediately at ease.

There was nothing fancy about the Texas town. It was practically a mirror image of the one he'd left behind in Montana. No wonder Angela had gravitated toward Rocky Ridge and felt at home there.

"I know," she said at a look from him. "I see the resemblance, too. I saw it that first night I stopped in Rocky Ridge. Felt it, too. The people are the same, warm and friendly. I still don't know why you wanted to stop here, though, instead of going on through to Grandpa's."

"You said your family does Christmas up big. I want to contribute my share."

She regarded him with obvious puzzlement. "You mean like some champagne or a couple of pies?"

He chuckled at the suggestion. "Knowing your grandfather, I'm sure he has the food and beverages pretty much under control. I was talking about presents."

"That's not necessary," she protested. "You don't even know the family that well. There's no need to be buying presents. No one will expect it. I only picked up a few last-minute things before I left Dallas."

"I want to," he insisted stubbornly. "You can help me pick out the right things." He glanced at her worriedly. "Or are you too tired? If this is too much for you, you can settle down in one of the restaurants and wait for me. The Italian one looks nice. I can smell the garlic clear out here.''

''You are not sticking me off in some restaurant while you shop,'' she retorted. ''I love picking out gifts. I can get a few more myself. Where do you want to start?''

He glanced up and down the street. There weren't more than a dozen stores, all decorated brightly. ''You pick. You know what they stock better than I do.''

''Let's start at Dolan's,'' she decided.

He glanced across the street at the shop with a dusty, ancient display and a forlorn string of colored lights drooping across the window. ''The drugstore?'' he asked doubtfully. ''I'm not settling for cheap perfume and some boxes of stale candy, darlin'.''

''Don't let the window fool you. It's been that way since way before I was born. Eli Dolan never saw any need to change it. Sharon Lynn runs the place now and she's stubbornly stuck with tradition. But it has the best milk shakes I've ever had. Made from scratch with real ice cream.''

''Angel, we're supposed to be shopping, not eating.''

Her expression turned sly. ''The baby's starved and milk is very good for his bones.''

He grinned at the ploy. ''Oh, in that case, we absolutely should have a milk shake.''

A bell over the door tinkled as they entered and

half a dozen people seated at the old-fashioned soda fountain turned to stare.

"You're on display, cowboy," she said with a wink as she led the way to the counter.

Clint endured the stares, nodded at the introductions and stewed when the stares transferred themselves pointedly to Angela's oversize belly. It was one thing for the family to be watching the two of them speculatively. It was quite another to have the whole darned town ready to spread gossip.

"Maybe this was a bad idea," he muttered, just as Sharon Lynn emerged from a back room with a beaming smile.

"Hey, you two," she said cheerfully. "I'll bet you're here for milk shakes."

"You bet," Angela said eagerly, "chocolate."

Sharon Lynn caught Clint's eyes. "You, too?"

Caught now, he gave in to the inevitable. "Absolutely."

"I thought you'd be over at White Pines by now. Janet called earlier. She said you were expected any minute."

"Mom and Dad probably are there. We got sidetracked by a little shopping," Angela said.

Sharon Lynn leaned over the counter. "I don't see any packages."

"Because this was our first stop," Clint said. "Sustenance for the ordeal ahead."

"Ah, I see. Then I'd better make these shakes double thick. The stores are jammed and everyone's patience is frayed. Christmas Eve shoppers tend to be desperate. You'll need your strength to compete with them.''

One by one the other customers drifted away, either anxious to finish their own last-minute shopping or eager to spread the news that Angela Adams was back home with a mysterious stranger in tow and a baby on the way.

''Don't worry about them,'' Sharon Lynn told him when Angela had left them alone to use the rest room. ''They're harmless. The Adams clan has been giving this town something to talk about for years now. It's practically a tradition.''

''I should have thought about that before I subjected her to this, though.''

''Forget it. We've long since learned to be thick-skinned, since we seem destined to provide so much entertainment. Angela's not upset. Why should you be?'' She regarded him speculatively. ''Unless you really care deep down about her feelings?''

''Of course, I do.''

She beamed as if he'd confessed to something far more telling. ''That's a start,'' she said, giving him a peck on the cheek before going to wait on a wide-eyed customer who was staring at them from the cosmetic counter across the store.

When Angela emerged from the back, he smiled at her ready-for-anything expression.

''You look as if you're preparing to charge into battle,'' he teased.

''Have you ever shopped on Christmas Eve before? It's full-scale warfare.''

''Even in Los Pinos?''

"Especially in Los Pinos. One of the other traditions around here is that everyone waits until the last minute to shop, so they can brag about how insane it was. I've seen people kicking and shoving to get the last electric razor."

"That bad, huh?"

"Worse," she insisted, then grinned. "But you have an edge. Practically nobody will argue with a pregnant lady."

"I just knew you were going to come in handy," he responded, then held out his hand. He studied her intently. "You're sure you're up to this?"

"Lead on. I can't wait."

Clint had never shopped for quite so many people before, not when he had a decent amount of money in his bank account and a heart that was suddenly full of Christmas spirit. Nor had he ever been accompanied before by a woman with a zealousness for a good bargain and the taste of an aristocrat.

They made four trips back to his pickup to deposit bundles of leather gloves, silver money clips and enough silk scarves to perform the dance of the seven veils. On the last trip, he suggested once again that Angela take time out and wait for him.

"No way," she argued. "I'm just getting warmed up. There's a sale at Geoffrey's we haven't checked out."

"You misunderstood, angel. That wasn't a suggestion. That was an order. Go have another milk shake. Rest. Gossip with your cousin. Geoffrey's, whatever that is, will wait."

"Geoffrey's is a dress boutique," she said distractedly. Her gaze clashed with his. "Why are you so anxious to get rid of me?"

"It's Christmas Eve and I'm shopping. Why do you think?"

Her expression brightened as his meaning finally registered. "Oh."

He saw her reach instinctively to her neck and guessed that she was wearing the pendant he'd given her the year before. He'd been wondering about that. He had noticed the gold chain and thought it was the same one, but he hadn't been able to detect whether the tiny tree was on it or whether it had been exchanged for something else. She always wore it carefully tucked beneath her blouse. Her unconscious gesture now was very telling. He gathered she hadn't wanted him to see that she was sentimental about anything connected to him.

Ah, well, let her have her secrets, he thought with a smile.

"Are you going to wait in the drugstore or in the truck?" he asked.

Her eyes sparkled mischievously. "Maybe I have shopping of my own to do."

"Then we'll meet back here in twenty minutes?"

"Twenty? You can pick out a present for me in twenty minutes?"

He enjoyed the fact that she sounded disgruntled. "I was thinking of grabbing the first suitable thing I came across," he teased. "Maybe a huge bottle of that perfume I saw Sharon Lynn selling to a customer earlier."

"I'm sure whatever it is will be lovely," she said

as primly and politely as any child who'd ever anticipated a doll only to receive socks and underwear.

"I'll do my best," he said cheerfully. "Twenty minutes, OK?"

"Fine. Don't get all bent out of shape if it takes me longer."

He noticed that she pointedly headed off in the direction of the hardware store. He also noticed that she kept glancing back over her shoulder to try to see where he was going. He waited until she finally went inside, her expression grimly determined, before moving swiftly up the block himself and going around the corner to a store he'd spotted earlier. He'd deliberately ignored it then, preparing for this moment and hoping that Angela wouldn't guess his destination.

It took him only a few awe-struck moments to make his selection and to arrange for a delivery to the ranch. At the mention of White Pines, the middle-aged clerk became even more accommodating.

"This is for Angie, then? I heard she was expecting a baby any minute."

The grapevine hadn't wasted a second, he noticed. "True enough."

"So," the woman said, "are you the proud daddy?"

Clint figured it wasn't any big secret, not at this point. "That's right."

"You're a lucky man. Angie was always a doll. I taught her English all through high school. I just moonlight here during the holidays. She had a real gift for understanding literature. I always thought she'd teach one day. I heard that's what she studied at college.''

Since she seemed to have more facts than he did about Angie's educational history, Clint kept silent. The clerk handed him his receipt. ''You have a real nice Christmas and tell Angie I said hello. Mrs. Grayson. She'll remember. Tell her I'd love to see her if she gets a minute while she's home.''

''I'll be sure and tell her,'' Clint agreed. ''Merry Christmas.''

He made one more stop en route back to the car and tucked that gift in his pocket. He was leaning against the side of the pickup in nineteen minutes. He noticed there was no sign of Angie.

He finally spotted her lugging an ungainly bundle down the block. She could barely see around it.

''What on earth?'' he asked, taking it from her and hoisting it into the bed of the truck. It wasn't as heavy as he'd expected, but it was the most oddly shaped package he'd ever seen. His curiosity stirred, despite his long-standing disinterest in gifts of any kind. Except for the gathering of relatives, holidays hadn't been a big deal at his house. Gifts had been practical, not sentimental or lavish. He'd never even seen, much less received anything that looked quite like this.

''Do I get a clue?'' he asked, eyeing the giant red package with its huge green bow.

She grinned. ''Do I?''

''I don't think so.''

''Then neither do you.''

"Just answer one question, then. Is it likely to explode?"

"Probably not," she said, her expression thoughtful. "Not if you drive very carefully."

"You know, angel, you're a real cutup."

"So they say."

He thought about passing along the message from her old high school teacher, then thought better of it. If he mentioned Mrs. Grayson, it was entirely possible that Angela would know where she moonlighted during the holidays. She might have been doing it for years. He would pass along the greetings tomorrow.

"Are you finished now?" Angela asked.

He glanced at the mound of packages tucked behind the seats of the truck. "I think so. I have something for your parents, all the aunts and uncles, the cousins and both housekeepers. That should do it, right?"

"Unless you're into pet toys, yes."

"Pets?"

"Dani has managed to foist off several kittens over the years. The main house is crawling with them, because Grandpa Harlan has always been a sucker for one of her sob stories. Uncle Jordan set a limit of two at home and he claims he's not happy about that, but I notice every time we're over there that one cat or another is always in his lap. Fortunately Dani's animal hospital also sells pet supplies and toys, so we buy them wholesale."

He shook his head. "Forgive me, but I think I'll skip presents for the cats."

"I'll forgive you," she said readily, then regarded him slyly. "Dani's a whole other story."

He sighed. "Where's the clinic?"

She grinned. "Just two streets down to the left. She'll be thrilled to see us."

"How many cats are we talking about?"

"Hard to say. The little devils multiply like rabbits."

"You'd think she'd do something about that. She is a vet, for goodness' sakes."

"She's also a soft touch. Every kid in town knows they can get a free kitten from her that's up-to-date on all its shots. She's the town's own personal animal shelter. There's no need for a pet store in Los Pinos."

Following Angela's directions, he pulled up in front of a small white house with dark green shutters. An old-fashioned white sign hung from a wrought-iron pole. A half-dozen cats lazed in patches of sunlight on the sloping front porch.

"The clinic entrance is on the side," Angela told him. "We can go in through the house and catch her in her office. Judging from the number of cars along here, half the pets in town have been overindulging in Christmas goodies. The waiting room will be a mess. Besides, family does have its privileges."

A harried-looking Dani barely waved at them as they slipped into the back of the clinic.

"Shopping for the cats," Angela called over the racket of barking dogs, howling cats and an occasional protesting screech from what sounded like a parrot or maybe a myna bird.

"A lot of pets get boarded here over the holidays," Angela told him. "I tried helping out once when I was in high school and Dani was still assisting Doc Inscoe during vacations from veterinary school. I couldn't stand it. Too much commotion. She's in heaven, though, and that's what matters. It was the only thing she ever wanted to do."

She led the way into what struck Clint as a pet store boutique. It was filled with elegant little sweaters for puppies, outrageously expensive leashes, dog houses that looked like mansions and a more varied assortment of toys than he'd ever imagined existed.

"Dani tends to indulge her animals. She thinks everyone else should, too. It's her little eccentricity, but we love her, anyway."

While he was still gaping in amazement, she zeroed in on several inexpensive little kitty treats hanging from an artificial tree like decorations. She gathered up a supply.

"I'll total up the cost at home and you can pay her when you see her," she said, dumping her selections into a bag and handing it to him.

"Are you sure this isn't a setup to get me arrested for shoplifting?" he inquired as they headed back through the house without so much as a parting wave for the clinic's owner.

"She won't even remember we've been here," Angela assured him. "Your money will come as a huge and welcome surprise."

Clint shrugged. "If you say so."

He added this package to all the others, then

helped Angela into the truck. "Is this it? Anything else you want to do here in town?"

She shook her head.

Clint started the truck, then glanced over and caught the faraway expression on her face.

"What is it?"

"It just sank in. You and I are actually going to White Pines. Together."

There was something in her eyes and in her voice that told him not to make light of that. "That means even more to you than me showing up at your folks' place, doesn't it?"

She nodded. "I can't really explain it. Our ranch is home, but White Pines is…" Her voice trailed off.

"Is what?" he prodded.

"Something special," she said eventually. "Our history, I guess. Just wait. You'll see. Grandpa's ranch is like no place else on earth."

Given the fact that her own family's ranch was pretty spectacular, that was saying something. "Big?" he asked, trying to pin it down.

"Our place is bigger actually. Luke was trying to make a statement. It's not the house or even the land. It's a feeling that comes over all of us there, a sense of our own history maybe. Home is home," she said, clearly struggling to explain so he would understand. "White Pines is our heritage."

Heritage wasn't something that had meant much to Clint growing up. He'd hoped to change that with his own small ranch. He'd envisioned it as a legacy he could pass on, one that would flourish and grow with succeeding generations. It was clear that Harlan

Adams and the generations preceding him had already endowed Angela and the others with that kind of meaningful legacy.

For one fleeting instant of doubt, he wondered if he would ever be able to offer her anything that would compare to it.

Chapter Ten

Clint and Angela's belated arrival at White Pines was greeted with amazement. Most of the family had already settled in and started helping Consuela and Maritza with the final preparations for tonight's family celebration and tomorrow's traditional open house but they all came out to help with the bundles that Clint had managed to amass in Los Pinos, exclaiming over the sheer number of them.

"I told you you were going overboard," Angela told him.

"What'd you do, son? Buy out the stores?" Grandpa Harlan asked with a grin.

He shot a look Angela's way, then said, "We tried, sir. Angela wore out too quickly."

"Very funny," she retorted. "Everything's

wrapped. The presents can go straight under the tree.''

"Except for the cat toys," Clint reminded her dryly.

"Oh, no, you didn't," her mother protested. "Tell me you did not make Clint buy gifts for all of your grandfather's cats."

"What can I say? He was feeling generous."

"And you took advantage," her mother chided, regarding Clint with sympathy. "Shame on you, Angela."

"Just doing my bit to keep Dani's business afloat," Angela insisted nobly. "She'd give away the store unless she's changed drastically."

Silence fell at what should have been no more than an innocuous comment. To Angela's confusion her mother rushed to change the subject.

Angela put her hand on her mother's arm to prevent her from leaving. She let the others lead Clint inside. As soon as they were out of earshot, she asked, "Mom, what's going on with Dani? I sensed something the other day, but Sharon Lynn hushed me up. Now everybody here gets all quiet when I so much as mention the possibility that she's changed."

"Sweetie, she's had a rough year, that's all," her mother said, looking decidedly uncomfortable. "I'm sure she'll tell you about it one of these days."

"Why don't you tell me and save her the trouble?" Angela suggested. "It might keep me from putting my foot in my mouth over and over again."

"It's her story to tell or keep to herself."

"Someone hurt her," Angela guessed. "Badly."

Her mother sighed. "Yes. Very badly. She lost three people she loved very much. Now let it go. Christmas is not the time for Dani to be thinking about the past. The best gifts you could give her are your love and support."

"And no questions," Angela surmised.

"Exactly."

She relented and kept the burgeoning questions to herself. She followed her mother inside. The rest of the family was gathered in the huge living room discussing the best place for the mound of gifts Clint had bought.

"We can't put them under the tree," Jenny protested. "It's not even decorated yet. We'll be stepping on them." Her dark eyes glinted with mischief. "I say we open them now."

"Nice try, you little sneak," Angela teased. "You always did want to open something on Christmas Eve. Next thing we knew you had half your presents open. It's time you learned to wait until morning like the rest of us. You're supposed to be grown-up, the oldest of all of us. It's about time you set an example."

"What's the fun of being grown-up at Christmas?" Jenny complained, poking at a particularly lumpy package with evident curiosity.

"You get to discover the joy of anticipation," Angela told her, then glanced at Clint. His steady gaze stirred its own brand of anticipation deep inside her. Aside from a couple of stolen kisses and a few fleeting, if very promising caresses, he'd barely touched her in too many months now. She knew all about the slow build of anticipation. Judging from the hunger she saw burning in his eyes, so did he.

She wondered idly if they could sneak in a kiss or two if she showed him the way to his room now. Her grandfather promptly put an end to that idea by suggesting a tour of the ranch before dark. Angela knew when it came to a competition between her and a herd of cows, it was a real toss-up which one would win. Clint reacted with predictable enthusiasm. Naturally Cody and Luke had to go along. Jordan stayed behind to make business calls.

"On Christmas Eve?" her grandfather grumbled. "What's wrong with you, boy? Don't you ever take a vacation?"

"When I do, it won't be to sightsee on a ranch I grew up on," Jordan retorted, grinning to soften the remark. "I'll whisk my beautiful wife off to a deserted beach in the Caribbean. You go chase after your cows. While I'm sitting in here by the fire, I promise I'll think of all of you out there freezing your butts off for no good reason."

After they'd gone and the women had retreated to the kitchen once again, Angela was left with her uncle. She wondered if Jordan would be any more forthcoming about Dani's troubles than her mother had been. Tales of his bemusement at becoming the adoptive father of a precocious five-year-old when he'd married Kelly were part of family legend. It was evident to anyone, though, that Jordan had taken to fatherhood and to Dani with the same kind of dedication that had built his oil empire.

"Uncle Jordan, can I ask you something before you make those calls?" Angela asked.

He glanced up distractedly from the pocket-sized computer that held the numbers of his important business contacts. "Sure, angel. What's up?"

"I'm worried about Dani. She hasn't seemed herself since I got back."

Normally the most tranquil of her relatives, Jordan suddenly looked mad enough to wring somebody's neck with his bare hands. "Leave it be," he said curtly.

"But—"

"Dammit, I said leave it alone," he thundered. "She's been through enough without dragging it all up again, OK? The holidays are going to be especially bad as it is, thanks to that fool idiot she fell for."

His fury stunned her into momentary silence. "I'm sorry," she said quietly, beginning to get the picture, though far from all of it. "I didn't mean to upset you."

His expression softened. "No, I'm the one who's sorry. I shouldn't be taking it out on you. I know you're just concerned about her. Please, please, just don't ask her about it. Can you promise me that?"

"Of course," she said at once.

To herself, though, she vowed to get at the bottom of Dani's troubles. The two of them had always been especially close. Four when Angela was born, Dani had prided herself on helping to care for her messy baby cousin. As they had grown up, Dani had always been as eager as she to get into mischief.

"You two are just natural-born trouble," her grandfather had said on more than one occasion. He'd always said it with more pride than venom, though. Grandpa Harlan admired spunk, even when it made mincemeat of the discipline their parents favored. They knew to save their most daring enterprises for visits to White Pines.

"What happened, Dani?" she murmured as she climbed the stairs to the room she'd always used on visits to White Pines. "What or who hurt you so?" Every instinct told her this went way beyond a simple broken romance.

For the first time since his arrival in Texas in search of Angela, Clint felt his old confidence soaring. Ranching was something he knew and loved every bit as much as the men who were riding over White Pines land with him. Like them, he appreciated the beauty of the land. Like them, he understood the complexities and hardships of the business and the excitement of mastering the daily challenges.

"You have an impressive operation here," he told Harlan and Cody.

"It wasn't always that way," Harlan told him. "My ancestors hadn't run the ranch the way they should have. It took a lot of time and hard work and pure cussedness to make it what it is today."

"You should have seen us trying to drag Daddy into the computer age," Cody said. "He still thinks those new-fangled machines will be the downfall of us all." He grinned at his father. "Am I quoting you accurately?"

"Pretty much," Harlan said. "I still say you're in a hell of a fix when the electricity goes out and everything you need to know about your operation is lost in some danged machine."

"That's why we have back-up disks and battery-powered laptops," Cody responded.

"More money wasted that could have been spent on a new bull for the herd," Harlan insisted.

"See what I mean?" Cody said. "He'd be happy if we still did the books in an old ledger."

"Come up to my place," Clint suggested. "I'm lucky if my receipts ever get entered into a ledger. By the time I get back to the ranch house at the end of the day about all I can cope with is falling into bed. You'd be in heaven."

"He would," Luke agreed. "What about it, Daddy? Want to go and rough it at Clint's? You can reminisce about the good old days."

Harlan scowled at his sons. "Now the two of you are trying to run me off my own place. That's the trouble with sons, Clint. Now daughters," he said with a sigh, "they're something else again. They give a man comfort in his old age."

Luke and Cody exchanged a look.

"He must have forgotten about Jenny stealing his pickup and crashing it into a tree," Cody said.

"And the time she ransacked the tool shed and splashed paint all over it," Luke added. "Then there was Lizzy's nosedive from the barn rafters. Broke her arm in two places."

"Selective memory," Cody agreed. "I hear it happens a lot in old folks."

"You think your sisters were trouble, maybe we should start dredging up the grief you all caused me," Harlan shot right back. "Let Clint weigh that and see whether he'd rather Angela delivered a girl or a boy."

Luke's expression softened at once. "Girls are a blessing," he admitted. "Angela could always light up a room. I'd come home at the end of an exhausting day and one smile on that little girl's face would cheer me right up."

"Indeed," Cody chimed in. "Sharon Lynn has been a joy compared to that brother of hers. Harlan Patrick must take after Daddy. He surely doesn't take after me."

"Who are you trying to kid?" Harlan demanded. "That boy is all your own worst sins come home to haunt you."

Clint chuckled at the nonstop and obviously affectionate banter. "Do you all ever let up on each other?"

"Never," Luke said.

"Why should we?" Cody asked. "Daddy acts as if we've made his life a torment, but there's another side to that story we could share with you."

"Never mind," Harlan said hurriedly. "We'd better be getting back and cleaned up before the women get dinner on the table. We'll never hear the end of it if we're late for Christmas Eve supper."

"Who cooked the turkey?" Cody asked worriedly. "Maritza or Janet?"

"I'm going to tell Janet you asked that," Harlan

swore. "You'll be lucky if you get out of here in one piece."

"When was the last time you ate anything she cooked?" Cody retorted.

His father grinned. "Not since I married her, I guarantee you that. When we were courting, I had to be polite. Fortunately, most of the time she had the good sense to try to sneak food in from some restaurant and pretend she'd fixed it."

"Now who's telling tales?" Luke asked. "Isn't a husband duty bound to gloss over all his wife's flaws in public?"

"This isn't public, Luke," Harlan declared. "Clint's practically part of the family."

"Well, I still say we should be setting an example for him," Luke protested. "The first time he gives away any of my daughter's little idiosyncrasies, I can just about guarantee there will be fireworks."

"Your daughter has idiosyncrasies?" Cody asked, feigning astonishment. "Since the day she was born, you've had us believing she was perfect."

"She is," Luke said quickly, then grinned. "For the most part." The grin quickly shifted to a scowl when he faced Clint. "That's something I can get away with saying, son. You can't. Just a word of caution."

"Believe me, that's advice I won't have any problem taking. I've seen your daughter's temper at close range." He gestured to a tiny slash over his lip. "Have the scars to prove it, too."

"She hit you?" Harlan asked incredulously.

"With a skillet," Clint claimed, though the truth

was even more humiliating. He'd actually walked straight into the danged thing while she was waving it around as a threat. "It pretty well ended the last discussion we had before she tore off and disappeared on me."

"You must have riled her pretty good."

Clint realized he'd just waltzed himself straight into a dangerous trap. Maybe they suspected the fight had been over Angela's pregnancy, maybe they didn't. It wasn't a topic he particularly wanted to discuss with them.

"The same way you all rile your wives, I suspect...by disagreeing with them," he said.

The response drew the expected laughter and the potentially tense moment dissipated. They were still laughing when they walked inside.

Angela looked up from the pie crust she was filling with pumpkin and promptly caught Clint's eye. She looked worried. He walked over and brushed a kiss across her lips, plainly startling her.

"There's nothing to worry about, angel. We were just doing a little male bonding."

"That's what worries me," she responded.

"Shouldn't you be sitting down to do that?" he asked, deliberately changing the subject. He reached for a chair. "Sit."

"It's easier if I stand."

They scowled at each other in a stubborn test of wills. Clint finally shrugged. "Suit yourself. I'm going up to shower and change."

"Supper's in an hour," she called after him.

"Then you'd better get upstairs, too. I've never known you to take less than that to get ready."

"Uh-oh," Luke and Cody muttered in unison.

"I'm out of here," Harlan said, patting Clint on the back as he passed. "Good luck, son. If you figure a way out of this one, let me know."

Their wives vanished right along with them, leaving Clint with only Consuela and Maritza to run interference. The two housekeepers took one look at Angela's stormy expression and muttered something in Spanish that sounded dire. Then they, too, retreated.

"Take it back," Angela said, advancing on him with a spoon covered with pumpkin.

"You wouldn't want me to lie now, would you?" he taunted, edging around the table and trying to keep it between them. He figured he was safe enough. She wasn't half as quick as she'd been the time she'd caught him off guard with that skillet.

"Who spends twenty minutes just polishing his boots?" she demanded. "And another twenty in the shower?"

"Do the math, angel. That still puts me ahead of you."

"We haven't even gotten to the amount of time you spend shaving and admiring yourself in the bathroom mirror."

"Are you suggesting I should grow a beard to save time dressing?"

"No. What I am suggesting, Mr. Brady, is that you are a bald-faced liar."

"Takes one to know one."

She paused at that. The spoon, which she'd been waving threateningly, drooped to her side. From across the room he couldn't be sure, but he thought there might be tears in her eyes.

"Angel?"

"What?" she asked with a telltale sniff.

"Don't cry."

"I am not crying, even if that was another particularly low blow."

He circled the table to reach her, ready to take her in his arms and kiss away the tears. She whapped him on the butt with that damnable spoon. When she would have done it again, he wrenched it away from her and pulled her into an embrace that stilled her frantic movements.

Gazing down into her upturned face, he saw that he had been right about the tears, but there were also glints of laughter sparkling in her eyes now as well.

"Got you, didn't I?" she said with obvious pride.

"Only because you're sneaky. Truce?"

She sighed and slid her arms around his waist and rested her head against his chest. "Truce," she murmured.

Clint felt a rare and unexpected surge of contentment steal over him as he held her.

"Think we can keep the truce through New Year's?"

"I doubt it," she said honestly.

He grinned. "Me, too."

She sighed again. "Clint?"

"Yes."

"Do you think that means we should give up on any idea of a future together?"

"Just because we can't go ten minutes without arguing?"

"Yes."

"I don't see why, as long as we have sense enough to stop and listen to each other occasionally. Some relationships are just plain volatile. It keeps the adrenaline pumping."

"Are you saying we're excitement junkies?"

"I suppose." He regarded her curiously. "Do your parents argue?"

"All the time," she admitted.

"Have you ever doubted their love for each other?"

"Never."

"See there," he said. "Maybe they'll tell us how they make it work."

"Sex," Angela said without hesitation, then blushed. "I mean I don't know this for a fact or anything. It's not something we discussed. Haven't you noticed, though, that they're always touching, always stealing a kiss when they think no one's looking?"

"Like us," Clint pointed out.

"At least the way we used to be," she said thoughtfully.

"You can't steal a kiss from someone who's run off to another state, angel."

She met his gaze evenly. "Point taken. No more running," she promised. "I swear to you that I will stay right here and try to work things out."

"You're making a commitment?" he asked, surprised by the renewal of the vow she'd made before coming to White Pines.

"A commitment to try," she amended. "It's not going to be easy, you know. There's a mountain of distrust between us."

"Our baby deserves nothing less than our best efforts," he responded. "He deserves to know that we've done everything possible to give him a real family."

"Everything," she echoed.

Clint pressed a kiss against her forehead. Anything more and neither one of them would have been ready for dinner on time. Of course, time wasn't the only thing frustrating them at the moment. This baby of theirs was a built-in warning to cool down.

As they went upstairs hand in hand, he couldn't help wondering, though, whether Angela would remember her promise tomorrow when she saw one of the gifts he had bought for her. Maybe he ought to give it to her now, when she was in such an amenable mood. In his experience it was best to capitalize on moments like these to pin her down about anything. A day from now, even an hour from now, the winds might be blowing another way entirely.

Chapter Eleven

Male bonding, indeed, Angela thought irritably.
They'd probably been out there conspiring to get her
married to Clint with the least amount of fuss.
They'd probably been indulgently listing all of her
idiosyncrasies and giving Clint advice on how to
cope with them. Men! Especially Adams men!

She hurriedly took her shower and rushed to get
dressed in a half hour, just to make the point that she
could move quickly when the situation called for
speed.

She thought back over the conversation they'd just
had. The truce she and Clint had declared was just
dandy. It would make the holidays peaceful.

But, she resolved, that didn't mean she wouldn't
put him in his place occasionally. After all, the
women in this family had to take a stand once in a

while or be completely run over by their stubborn, willful and thoroughly unpredictable mates.

Goodness knows, she would never have guessed that both her father and her grandfather would take such an immediate shine to Clint, despite their natural protectiveness of her. They seemed to understand the man who'd tracked her down all the way from Montana. They talked the same language—ranching and testosterone. Clint was becoming one of the family before she could spit. On the one hand, she could see the benefits of that. On the other, it was darned annoying.

To her surprise, Clint seemed to be settling in quite nicely. He was showing no inclination to duck out and run home, no matter how she infuriated him. He seemed to have made up his mind to stick this out.

In fact, instead of being scared off, he seemed to be endlessly fascinated with everything about her and her family. And, if the truth be told, he also seemed every bit as intrigued by her swollen body as he had been on the day they'd met, back when she'd actually had a figure to brag about. For a woman who was feeling especially ungainly that alone would have been enough to endear the man to her.

She was also beginning to understand just how deeply she'd hurt him by taking off as she had. His anger over having missed so much of her pregnancy appeared genuine. Her heart just ached, thinking about all they could have shared if she hadn't denied them the chance by running away. Every time she turned around she saw fresh evidence of the kind of devoted father he would be, the kind of father any child would be blessed to have.

In fact, to her very deep regret, she was beginning to weaken. She was beginning to recall just why she'd fallen in love with the man in the first place. He was kind and gentle and amazingly patient. For the most part, anyway.

His touches made her sizzle from the inside out. And his kisses could have ignited a bonfire in a soaking rain.

But that didn't mean she would marry him…if that was what he was after with this truce. He hadn't actually said the words, not lately, not since that impulsive declaration he'd made when he'd first arrived. His entire focus seemed to be on the baby she was carrying.

In the dead of night, when she was feeling restless and uncomfortable, she couldn't shake the very real possibility that his child was all he really wanted, that when the baby came he'd fight her for custody. He'd hinted at that often enough. In fact, he'd virtually threatened her with the possibility.

Still, in the past couple of days, aside from an occasional verbal dig, they had pretty much managed to put all her lies behind them. The truce had sealed their pact to leave the past in the past. It was either a terrific start or the greatest lie of all, made to lull her into a false sense of complacency. Was it possible he meant only to win her trust, then abandon her, as she had him?

As she ran a brush quickly through her hair and dashed on a hurried dusting of makeup, she wondered if the risks of this truce didn't outweigh the benefits. Maybe it would be smart to start building a wall between them, one that would protect her when the inevitable time came for him to go, and the fighting started over their child.

She wasn't sure she would be able to bear that kind of ugly battle. She feared, too, that when the whole truth came out about how she'd deceived Clint, her family would desert her and support him. They were all honorable people and Clint was bound to have their sympathy on his side.

She was an Adams, though, she reminded herself sternly. That still counted for something. Even if every one of her relatives disapproved of what she'd done, they would back her in any kind of struggle for her child. She had no choice but to believe that they would fight to claim an Adams heir, no matter the circumstances of his conception.

She looked at her watch and grinned. Forty minutes precisely. She cast one last glance in the mirror and nodded approvingly. The dark green velvet maternity dress she wore was the perfect foil for her pale skin and auburn hair. The pendant Clint had given her rested between her breasts, drawing attention to their new lushness. She concluded she looked about as sensual and provocative as it was possible for an eight-and-a-half-months-pregnant blimp to look.

She also squared her jaw and stiffened her resolve. She would maintain Clint's truce, because she had promised, but she would keep her own defenses squarely in place.

"Remember that," she said sternly as she reached for the knob to open her door with fifteen minutes to spare.

Confident that she'd done the impossible in getting ready so quickly, she hurried downstairs and walked toward the living room.

To her chagrin, Clint was there before her, wearing a well-tailored suit and silk tie that had her gaping. He was a handsome man in denims and flannel. In a charcoal gray suit with his hair tamed, he was devastating. She couldn't help wondering if he'd brought that suit along because Christmas was coming or because he intended it to be his wedding suit. Her pulse fluttered wildly and her determination flew out the window. It either proved just how weak her resolve was or how extraordinarily potent he was.

His gaze locked with hers and she gravitated toward him across the room as if he were reeling her in with some invisible line.

"You look incredible," she admitted. "I've never seen you in a suit before."

"There's not a lot of call to wear one when I'm out with the cattle." His gaze swept over her appreciatively. "You've never put on such a fancy dress before, either. The color becomes you. You should wear it all the time."

It was the longest and prettiest compliment he'd ever paid her. Another brick thumped out of her recently erected and still-uncertain wall of defenses.

"Would you like something to drink?" he asked. "Harlan's brought in some nonalcoholic champagne just for you."

"I'd love a glass," she said, hoping it would take him a very long time to pour it. She could spend the time gathering her composure.

"It's a good sign when you can get a man to wait on you," Sharon Lynn teased, coming over to stand beside her. "It means he's totally, thoroughly smitten."

"Does Kyle Mason wait on you?" Angela asked, then regretted it when she saw the sad expression on her cousin's face.

"He doesn't even know I'm alive," Sharon Lynn confessed irritably, then sighed. "It's humiliating. I've tried flirting. I've tried making him double-rich shakes when he stops by the drugstore. I've even considered asking him out, but my pride balks at that."

Glad to have her own relationship sidelined as the topic of conversation, Angela asked, "Who is he? He didn't go to school with us, did he?"

"No. He's new to the area. He turned up about six months ago."

"And just how often does this Kyle Mason come into Dolan's?"

"Every day or so," Sharon Lynn said.

"And where's his ranch?"

"About thirty miles north of Los Pinos. He bought the old Carlson spread at Cripple Creek."

Angela grinned. "Doesn't that strike you as a long drive to take so frequently if the man hasn't noticed you? Unless, of course, he's addicted to milk shakes," she added.

Sharon Lynn paused, her expression thoughtful. "I

never thought about that. Do you think that's possible?''

"Likely, in fact. Maybe he's just shy," Angela suggested. "And the Adams name might be intimidating to a newcomer around here. Could be you're going to have to take the initiative. Call him right now and invite him to the open house tomorrow."

"I couldn't," Sharon Lynn protested.

"Why not?"

"Last-minute invitations are so tacky."

"Not to someone who's been waiting and waiting for you to make a move."

"He probably has plans."

"Stop making excuses, Sharon Lynn," Angela chided. "You won't know unless you call. At least it'll signal him that you're interested."

Her cousin's expression brightened. "I'm going to do it," she said, heading determinedly for the privacy of Grandpa Harlan's office.

"What was that all about?" Clint asked, reappearing with the champagne.

"You didn't listen in?"

"Of course not. It sounded like private girl talk."

Amused by his sudden burst of discretion, she said, "It was. I was just trying to shove my cousin off an emotional bridge."

"Uh-oh," he said uneasily. "Are you sure there's going to be somebody underneath to catch her?"

"Pretty sure."

"What if she gets the wrong answer and it ruins her holidays?"

She scowled at him. "Do you always have to look at the dark side of things?"

"Just being realistic."

Before Angela could worry herself into a tizzy over having inadvertently set Sharon Lynn up for a miserable holiday, her cousin dashed back into the room, her face aglow.

"He said yes," she practically shouted across the room. Oblivious to the curious glances from her parents and everyone else, she threw her arms around Angela. "Can you believe it? He said he would love to come. He didn't even hesitate."

"Obviously he'd been hoping for this."

"I was so sure he would have other plans. I know of at least three women in town who have been pursuing him like crazy."

"Other than you?" Angela teased.

"I have not been pursuing him," Sharon Lynn protested. "I have been very demure."

The thought of the exuberant Sharon Lynn as demure was enough to bring a smile, but Angela managed to keep a straight face. "Well, it looks as if that tactic has paid off, then," she said.

"Thank you for prodding me into doing something, anything, to get this relationship off dead center."

"Speaking of dead center," Clint interjected, his hand on Angela's shoulder. "Could I speak to you for a minute privately, before we go into dinner?"

She stared into his serious eyes and gulped. Either he was going to lecture her on interfering in Sharon Lynn's life or he had something much more personal in mind. She was well aware of the gaps already created in her defenses after no more than a few minutes in his company. A little time alone and she might as well kiss her resolve goodbye.

"Can't it wait?"

"Not really."

She heaved a sigh and gestured toward her grandfather's office. "Let's go in there. We'll be able to hear when the others start into the dining room."

With Sharon Lynn's fascinated gaze following them, they slipped away. Clint closed the office door firmly behind them. The soft click of the lock sent goose bumps dancing up her spine.

Vaguely alarmed, her gaze flew to his face. "What on earth was that for?"

"I don't want to be disturbed. There's only one way I can think of around here to manage that."

She instinctively backed up a step. "You're making this sound awfully serious."

"It is."

She saw him reach into his pocket, but even then his intentions didn't register. Not until he withdrew a small square package wrapped in gold did she begin to get an idea of what was on his mind. If he'd been determined to hit on a surefire way to destroy her resistance, this was it.

Angela swallowed hard and eyed that package as warily as if it were a rattler. "Shouldn't we wait until morning for presents?" she asked without much hope of him taking the suggestion. Obviously he'd planned the timing of this moment very carefully.

"Not this one," he insisted, holding it out in the

palm of his hand. He grinned at her. "Take it, angel. It won't bite."

She plucked it out of his hand as gingerly as if it might explode. She fingered the curling gold ribbon, but made no move to untie it.

"Come on," he urged. "Open it."

She lifted her gaze to his. "I'm afraid to," she admitted candidly.

He regarded her with obvious astonishment. "Why?"

"I don't think I can explain it."

"Try."

"If..." She drew in a deep breath, then tried again. "If it's what I think it is, it will change things."

"Forever," he agreed.

She sighed and closed her eyes. "That's what I was afraid of. Clint, we just declared a truce. It's too soon to ask for anything more."

He regarded her with amusement. "It's not as if we just met, angel. This day has been a long time coming. Too long, some would say, including you, I thought."

If only he had done this back in Montana, she thought, then chided herself for being unreasonable. She hadn't given him a chance to. That didn't change the fact that it felt all wrong now.

"I know what you're trying to do," she began.

"Oh, really?" he said wryly. "What am I trying to do?"

"Make things right. Be responsible."

"And that's so terrible?"

"Clint, the timing is all off."

"What the hell is that supposed to mean?" he demanded, amusement giving way to exasperation.

She struggled for an explanation, but none came to her, none that would make sense to him anyway. "I can't explain. I'm sorry." She held out her hand, the unopened present still resting in her palm.

After an endless hesitation, he reached for the package, his disappointment plain. "Maybe you're right," he said halfheartedly. "I just thought..."

"I know what you wanted to do," she said. "And it was a lovely gesture, something I'll remember every single Christmas Eve as long as I live." She smiled, a little too brightly, probably. "I'm sure you can get your money back. The stores in Los Pinos have very lenient return policies."

That familiar headstrong look was back in his eyes. "I'm not taking it back to the store, angel. Just so you know, I'm going to do everything in my power to see that you accept it sooner or later."

She shuddered at the grim determination in his voice. If only he'd sounded like a man in love, instead of a man on a mission, she thought wistfully. Then it might have been almost impossible for her to say no.

Clint was disappointed, but not broken by Angela's refusal to so much as look inside that box, much less accept the proposal he'd been planning all day. Maybe it had been premature. It was just that he was so blasted anxious to get things settled once and for all. He wasn't used to being so out of control, to having anyone tie him in knots the way she did. He'd hoped to seize control back again.

Which, of course, was exactly the problem. They both wanted to set the ground rules and determine the pace of this relationship. What neither of them seemed willing to admit was that a third person was really in charge, that baby of theirs. If Clint had to hog-tie Angela and drag her in front of a minister, they were going to be man and wife when that baby was born.

As soon as he and Angela had rejoined the others, he realized that he'd made a mistake in asking for that moment alone with her. He should have caught up with her upstairs or waited. Now he'd raised expectations that the two of them would be making an announcement over dinner. He could see the anticipation in Harlan's eyes and the anxiety in Luke's and Jessie's. Jessie's gaze kept drifting to Angela's left hand as if she were expecting to see an engagement ring there.

"Dinner is ready," Maritza announced, saving him and Angela from the speculative glances.

"Luke, why don't you escort your daughter in tonight?" Harlan suggested. "Clint, you take Jessie."

Clint met Jessie's eyes and caught the spark of amusement.

"He wants to give me time to cross-examine you," Jessie said. "Subtlety is not Harlan's strong suit."

"You can always ask me anything. I'm an upfront kind of man. It saves wear and tear on the emotions."

"OK, then. Did you ask Angela to marry you tonight?"

"I did," he confirmed. "She said no."

Jessie sighed. "I thought as much. I just don't understand that daughter of mine. I can see perfectly plainly that she is crazy in love with you. She's just being stubborn, like a typical Adams. She got a double dose of it, too, with Erik's genes and Luke's influence."

"Being an Adams can't be all bad," Clint teased. "You signed on for it twice."

"True," she admitted with a rueful grin. "I suppose I'm every bit as stubborn as they are. I hung in there with Luke when he flatly refused to admit how he felt about me. I hope you'll do the same with Angela."

"I don't have a choice. She's carrying my child."

Jessie studied him worriedly. "Is that what you've been telling her?"

"More or less. Why?"

"Well, no wonder she turned you down," she said, regarding him with dismay.

"I want that baby of mine to have my name."

Apparently he'd raised his voice, because several of the others glanced their way.

"My father left us the day I was born," he said more quietly, but just as fiercely. "I grew up thinking it was my fault he was gone. I will not allow that to happen to a child of mine."

Jessie rested her hand on his. "I know you mean well. I can see that you're desperate to do right by

your baby, but what about Angela? How do you feel
about her?''

As he was about to respond, she silenced him with
a touch of her finger against his lips. ''Don't tell me.
Tell her.''

The message was plain as day and Clint wondered
how he could have been so blind to the obvious up
until now. Of course Angela wanted to know how he
felt about her. The only trouble was, he wasn't sure
of that himself.

Her betrayal loomed between them and no matter
how hard he tried, he couldn't seem to get beyond
it. He was still attracted to her. He still wanted her.
He understood the importance of forgiveness, but he
wondered if he was capable of it.

He was quiet through most of dinner, wrestling
with his conscience and his heart. He could have
been eating sawdust for all the attention he paid the
meal.

Beside him, Angela was just as quiet. She spoke
only when she was asked a direct question, and the
others, sensing that she was in turmoil, asked her
very little.

Fortunately, the Adamses were a boisterous crowd.
They more than made up for the silence of two of
the guests. Only when the time came to decorate the
tree did they insist on sweeping Clint and Angela
into the midst of the activity.

''I'm a little tired,'' Angela protested. ''I'll just sit
here and supervise.''

''Not a chance,'' Justin said, hauling her to her
feet. ''You're the only one who likes as many lights

as I do. The others would stop after a couple of wimpy strands.''

Clint observed in amusement as Angela and Justin wrapped at least eight strands of brightly colored lights around the tree. Watching them reminded him of her excitement just one year ago when he'd managed to find all those lights for their first tree together.

"Plug it in,'' Angela commanded now. When the lights blinked on, her eyes lit up. "It's beautiful.''

"It's blinding,'' Sharon Lynn declared. "We won't even be able to see to put the rest of the ornaments on.''

Angela rolled her eyes. "OK, OK. Turn 'em off, Justin. Let's finish decorating before we have the final lighting ceremony.''

Tall and awkward, with the stretched-out lankiness of adolescence, Jordan's son practically upended the tree as he reached for the plug.

As Clint grabbed the tree and righted it, his gaze caught Angela's. Suddenly they were connected as surely as if they'd hopped aboard a time travel machine and zoomed back twelve months. He could see the memory in her eyes. Her expression softened, her complexion glowed and her lips curved into the faintest suggestion of a smile. He remembered it all as if it were yesterday.

"Let them finish,'' he suggested softly, holding out his hand. "Before one of them tangles a strand of garland around your neck and chokes you.''

"Hey,'' Justin protested. "We're not that clumsy.''

"Couldn't prove it by me," Harlan Patrick taunted. "Who dropped one entire box of ornaments when we were carrying them down from the attic?"

Justin shot back a rude remark.

"Maybe I'd better sit down," Angela said, taking Clint's outstretched hand.

Though there were plenty of chairs in the room, Clint led her to a love seat so he could sit beside her. As carols played on the stereo and the cousins bickered and laughed, he felt a longed-for contentment steal over him again. When he turned Angela and settled her back against his chest, she didn't protest. Instead, to his relief, she sighed happily.

"Glad to be home?" he asked quietly.

She nodded. "But I miss Montana, too."

"You do?" Clint asked, surprised by the admission.

"Just the two of us. It was magical." She gazed up at him, her expression wistful. "I thought we were starting our own traditions."

"I thought so, too."

"Who would have thought so much would happen to change everything?"

"It doesn't have to," he said. "We can have that again, if we want it badly enough. Do you?"

Before she could answer, they were surrounded by cousins.

"Come on, Angie. You have to put the angel on top of the tree. It's tradition," Harlan Patrick said.

She gazed at Clint, her expression clearly torn.

"Go," he told her. "Traditions are meant to be carried on."

He sat back and watched as the others handed her the gold and white angel for the top of the tree. She handled the obviously expensive, obviously old angel with such tenderness that it brought an unexpected sting to Clint's eyes. There had been no such traditions in his family, no such sentiment. His mother had tried, but there were often too many divisions and old hurts to make the holidays anything but stressful. He'd stopped going home after a while.

He watched nervously as Justin helped Angela up the small ladder at the side of the huge tree, then steadied her as she reached for the top branch. She settled the angel firmly in place, then stepped down.

Someone with a magician's sense of timing turned on the tree lights at precisely the same moment as someone else doused the other lights in the room. There were audible gasps of delight, then applause.

"The best tree ever," Harlan declared.

"You say that every year, Grandpa," Justin teased.

"And every year it is the best," his grandfather retorted. "This year's best of all because the angel's back on top."

Angela stared at her grandfather. "I don't understand."

"He wouldn't let us put it on while you were gone," Sharon Lynn explained. "He said it was your job."

"I begged and begged," Lizzy complained, "but Daddy said we'd just have to wait till you came home again to see the angel back on the tree."

"Oh, Grandpa," Angela said, throwing her arms around his neck.

"Now, don't go getting all weepy on me, girl. You'll mess up my suit before church," he protested, looking pleased just the same.

Clint fingered the ring box that was still in his pocket and tried not to feel an overwhelming sense of defeat. How could he compete with this much love, with this family?

He realized then that Angela's gaze had sought out his. Their eyes met and lingered. His heart thundered in his chest at the desire and longing he thought he saw in her face. For just that instant, anyway, it seemed that no one else in the room mattered.

Possibilities stirred to life again inside him. Confidence soared. He found himself smiling. After all, this was the season of miracles, wasn't it? She'd said that herself not so long ago. Maybe one really was possible for the two of them.

Chapter Twelve

Angela hadn't been inside a church since she'd left home. It wasn't that she'd lost her faith; maybe it was just one more act of rebellion. At any rate, when she walked back into the small, candlelit church she'd attended for most of her life, she felt a sense of peace stealing over her. Subconsciously she reached for Clint's hand. The warmth of his grasp was even more reassuring.

Throughout the familiar Christmas Eve service, she was all too aware of the man beside her, his deep voice blending with hers as they sang the joyous hymns: "Silent Night," "The First Noel," "Joy to the World." Each one brought back memories of past holiday seasons; each one stirred thoughts of one particular Christmas in Montana.

Ever since that moment when their gazes had

locked back at White Pines, she had felt as if she and Clint were caught up in a spell. It was as if some unseen hand were drawing them closer and closer, insisting that they search their hearts for answers to the dilemma they faced.

She wanted to love him again, as freely as she had in Montana, without so many complications.

But life was filled with unexpected and unalterable twists and turns. Coping with them, in the end, would make them and their love stronger. She couldn't go back to being Hattie Jones, no matter how desperately she wanted to recapture that carefree time in her life. She was about to become a mother, with all the responsibilities—and joys—that entailed.

It would be so much easier to share the demands with someone, she thought wistfully, so much more meaningful to share the joys.

She stole a glance at the man beside her. Every line in his face, every expression on his lips was as dear and familiar to her as if they'd spent a lifetime together, rather than a few short months. Here was someone who wanted to take on that duty, who was eager to be a father to his son or daughter. On that score at least, she had come to trust Clint without reservation over the past few days. He loved the baby she was carrying as deeply as she did.

Tell me what to do, she prayed. *Please show me the path to take.*

There were no blinding messages in response, no signals in the night sky as they made their way home again. Maybe, as she had accused Clint of doing earlier, she was rushing things, trying to force a resolution when the only real answers would come with time. Patience, never one of her virtues, was absolutely necessary with so much on the line.

At home, when everyone else climbed up the steps to their rooms, Clint lingered at the foot of the stairs, his steady gaze on her.

"Sit with me awhile," he suggested. "By the tree."

As tired as she was, she was unable to resist the appeal of the invitation, the draw of the man uttering it.

The lights were still on, blinking reds and greens, blues and golds, a magnificent display of shimmering Technicolor. Leaning back in his arms, she half closed her eyes to soften the effect into something reminiscent of an Impressionist painting.

"What is it about a Christmas tree that makes us feel as if we've been touched by magic?" she asked.

She could tell from his thoughtful expression that he took the question seriously, and she loved him for that. Some men would have laughed it off as romanticized nonsense. Clint had always taken her most whimsical statements seriously, though. He was also capable of wicked wit or off-the-cuff philosophy. Their conversations had never been boring.

"It takes us back to childhood, maybe," he said. "Back to a time when we were truly innocent and filled with anticipation."

"Back to a time when we were greedy little brats, you mean."

He laughed. "I was trying for a positive spin."

"Do you ever think about what our baby will be like?"

He seemed startled by the shift in topic. "You mean boy or girl?"

"No, I mean the kind of person he or she will grow up to be. Does it scare you, thinking about what the world is like and how to protect him?"

"Or her," he reminded her. "Now, having a girl scares me more than a boy. I figure I won't want any daughter of mine to date until she's ninety for fear she'll run across a man like me."

"What's wrong with you?"

"You, of all people, have to ask?"

"You're strong. You're decent. You're intelligent. Any woman would be lucky to have you," she declared with feeling, then recognized the irony.

"May I remind you that a very short time ago you turned down my proposal before I could even get it out of my mouth," he said, obviously aware of the irony, too. "I'd rehearsed the darned thing, too."

"Want to say it now?" The suggestion was made only half in jest. A part of her wanted a chance to say yes, even if common sense told her to stay silent.

He studied her intently, then shook his head. "Not right this second, angel. I can't take being humiliated twice in one night."

"I'm sorry."

"Don't be sorry. I was being impulsive. You were trying to use good sense. Marriage isn't something to jump into for the wrong reasons."

He rested his hand on her belly, and Angela felt her pulse skitter crazily. His expression turned awestruck as the baby shifted inside her. When he lifted his gaze to hers, she was almost certain she detected the sheen of unshed tears.

"Though this is a pretty darned good reason for getting married, if you ask me," he said quietly.

It was, Angela agreed to herself. But it wasn't the one she desperately wanted to hear. She could have told him that, probably should have, but she didn't. She wanted him to recognize their love on his own, to admit to it without any prodding from her...if he could.

"I think I'll go up to bed now," she said instead. She stood up, then bent down to drop a kiss against his cheek. "Good night, Clint. Merry Christmas."

He captured her face between his hands and kissed her back, slowly, persuasively until her knees were so weak she could barely stand. If he'd meant to make a point, if he'd meant to remind her that the passion between them burned hot even now, then he had.

"Merry Christmas, angel," he murmured. "See you in the morning."

With her blood pumping fast and furiously through her veins, she regretted the decision to leave, but pride wouldn't let her turn back. That was the trouble with the two of them, she concluded. They both had pride to spare, but no one with whom to spend the night.

Christmas morning dawned cold and bright. Sun glistened on a fresh covering of snow that had fallen after they'd gotten home from church the night before. Clint had caught a glimpse of it when he'd finally gone up to his room.

He'd stood by the window for an eternity, staring out at the stark, rugged terrain of White Pines softened by its blanket of white. Oddly enough, he'd felt no envy. His own ranch might be smaller, less ostentatious, but he owned every acre of it free and clear. He could take pride in the work he had done to make it a thriving cattle operation, one that would grow over time.

Was it enough to offer a child, though? Especially a child who could have at least some small stake in all this someday? He didn't like the doubts that kept creeping in when he least expected them. He didn't want to think about going home without his son or daughter.

He didn't want to think about going without Angela.

It was strange. He had come to Texas in search of Hattie—or more precisely, the child he'd fathered—but he'd found a different woman entirely. Not just in name, but in demeanor and more. To be sure, her body had changed with the child she carried, but it ran deeper than that. Hattie had been flirtatious and loving and generous, but he'd never seen the strength in her that he saw in Angela. She was prepared to face the uncertain future on her own, if she had to, without him.

His own feelings had changed over the past few days, as well. He'd come after a child. His child. He'd stayed, at least in part, because of a woman. She intrigued him in ways that Hattie never had.

Only one thing had stayed the same; the hunger she could build in him with just a glance. The skim of her fingers across his flesh, the touch of her lips, and he was achingly hard and hot as a branding iron.

Those thoughts of permanence and forever were coming more and more frequently, buoyed by the notion that the foundation was more solid. His attraction to her had deepened into something that could last through time. And this time, he thought, they had the truth on their side. They had a fresh chance to get it right.

He thought about what Jessie had told him earlier about a woman needing to know that a man wanted her for herself and not for the baby she carried. Maybe it was time he admitted that, put his heart on the line. Not doing so up until now had been a coward's act. When Angela had turned his proposal down she'd refused an offer only slightly better than a business proposition. If he told her he cared, if he confessed to loving her, it would be him she was rejecting. Little had ever frightened him before, but that did.

He'd had a lot of months to toughen his pride. He'd had that final scene between them to play over and over again. He'd had the night she'd given him the slip in Montana to reinforce all of his fears that the woman he was chasing didn't want him. Just as his father hadn't. Old insecurities that had festered for years came back to haunt him.

He had no proof, none at all, that her feelings toward him had changed. Not really. Oh, she had returned his kisses with a matching ardor. She had sent glances his way that could steam up a mirror two rooms away. That should have been reassurance enough.

But Angela was unpredictable in ways that Hattie hadn't been. Telling her how he felt still seemed risky. The knowledge she would have after such an admission would give her a certain kind of power over him, and he didn't like giving anyone around him an edge they could turn against him.

He'd wrestled with the dilemma most of the night. By dawn the answers were no clearer than they had been.

He could sense that others were stirring. He'd checked with Consuela the night before, and she'd assured him that his gift for Angela had arrived and been safely hidden. It would be under the tree by this morning. Just thinking of it made him smile.

He rushed through his shower, dressed in another suit and struggled with another damnable tie. He'd be glad when the holidays ended and he could go back to wearing comfortable denims and flannel shirts again. He'd noticed that the other men had been complaining good-naturedly about their own fancy clothes the night before. Except for Jordan. He was a man who looked as if he'd been born to wear pinstripes. He was as relaxed in Armani as the rest of them were in their Levi's and Wranglers.

He thought of that soft, green velvet dress that Angela had worn the night before. It had taken every bit of his strength to keep from caressing the fabric and the woman wearing it. He supposed wearing a fancy suit once in a while was a small price to pay to see the women gussied up in velvet and silk and diamonds. Seeing the pendant he had given her nestled between her breasts had made him smile.

Pausing outside Angela's door now, he listened for sounds of her stirring, but heard nothing. He realized why, when he got downstairs. She was in the living room with her grandfather, Justin and young Harlan. They were all dressed up and staring avidly at the mound of packages under the tree.

"Merry Christmas, everyone," Clint said, not even trying to hide his amusement.

"Merry Christmas, son," Harlan said. He eyed Clint hopefully. "Did you hear anyone else stirring up there?"

"Not really. I just heard you all coming downstairs."

Four faces reflected obvious disappointment. Clint noticed that Angela's gaze was fixed on the huge, wrapped package tucked back in one corner. From its size, Clint guessed it had to be the one he'd bought for her. He picked out the huge, lumpy present she'd chosen for him, then returned his gaze to her.

"Curious, angel?" he inquired, taking a seat beside her.

"It's Christmas morning. Of course I'm curious."

"We could open just one package each," Harlan suggested. "Wouldn't be anything wrong with that, would there?"

"Grandpa, you know the others would kill us," Justin said. "The rule is we wait until everybody's up."

Harlan grinned. "Then the two of you go upstairs and raise a ruckus. Let's see if we can't get this show on the road."

When the two young men had raced off, Angela regarded him sternly. "Grandpa, you're worse than they are."

"There's nothing like the spirit of giving to perk up a man's day. I'm old. I have the right to indulge my kinfolk."

"Who are you trying to kid?" she teased. "You want to see what everyone got for you."

"Watch it, girl, or that present with your name on it just might vanish before we get to the unwrapping."

"He always threatens us like this," Angela told Clint. "The man threatened to take back my teddy bear one year."

"You told me the one you had at home was bigger. I figured you didn't need two. Also thought you needed to learn something about gratitude. You learned your lesson, didn't you?"

She grinned at him. "Yes, Grandpa," she said dutifully. "I think I'll go tell Consuela and Maritza we want to eat breakfast before we open packages. I'll suggest a nice, long, leisurely breakfast, pancakes, waffles, the works."

"Oh, no, you don't," he said, catching her hand when she would have sashayed past him. He turned his gaze on Clint. "Take her for a walk, will you? Keep her out of mischief until the others come down."

Clint glanced outside worriedly. "I don't know,

sir. It looks awfully cold and slippery out there. There's more snow coming down, too."

"Traitor," Harlan taunted. "I guess I'll go up and see if my wife is awake."

"Let her sleep if she's not," Angela said. "Yesterday was a long day. Today will be, too."

"Then she can catch up on her beauty sleep tonight, not on Christmas morning."

When he'd gone, Angela shook her head. "He always was the first one up on Christmas morning. He said he loved seeing our faces when we sneaked down the stairs to see if Santa had come."

"Who was second?" Clint asked.

"Me," she admitted. "Jenny always tried to act blasé and Dani was a sleepyhead. I didn't get any real competition until Sharon Lynn was big enough to get down the stairs by herself."

"Which just shows that some things never change," the woman in question said, yawning as she joined them. "Has anyone made coffee yet?"

"There's a pot on the buffet in the dining room," Angela said.

"I'll get it," Clint offered. "I could use a cup myself. Angel, what about you? Is there decaf?"

"I already have my herbal tea," she told him, lifting the mug to demonstrate.

He left the two of them poking at packages. They were still at it when he returned with the coffee and a huge tray of freshly baked sweet rolls Consuela had told him were meant to tide them over until after the presents had been opened.

One by one the others straggled down the stairs,

as Angela and Sharon Lynn waited impatiently. Harlan was grumbling when he returned, decrying Janet's determination to shower and dress before joining them.

"I've given that woman enough fancy robes to stock a lingerie shop. Couldn't she have worn one of them?" he complained.

"Maybe she figured that once this day gets rolling, she wouldn't have another chance. No woman owns a robe that's fancy enough for greeting guests. What time are people expected for the open house?" Angela asked.

"Noon, same as always."

"How many?" Clint asked.

"Not too many this year," Harlan said. "A hundred or so."

The whole town of Rocky Ridge wasn't much bigger than that, Clint thought. Yet Harlan was more nonchalant about entertaining for such a crowd than Clint would have been at fixing dinner for four. Of course, with Consuela and Maritza on the job, he probably had very little to do except stay out of the way.

It was twenty minutes before Janet came downstairs. A cheer went up.

"Finally," Harlan said, feigning exasperation. There was too much love shining in his eyes for the comment to have much bite to it. She settled on the carpet at his feet and rested her head against his thighs. His weathered hand settled gently on her head. There was no mistaking how they felt about each other, Clint thought, envying them.

Lizzy deemed herself Santa and parceled out packages with enthusiasm. For all of the insistence on waiting until everyone was downstairs, there was no organized system to the opening. Everyone shredded paper as fast as they could. Shouts were exchanged. Thanks were hollered back and forth. The excitement in the room was palpable.

Clint was startled when the first gift was pressed into his hands, stunned when several more were added. He was relieved that he'd insisted on shopping for everyone, including the cats who were getting tangled up in the scattering of ribbons as they chased wads of wrapping paper.

He saved Angela's present to him for last, then laughed aloud when he saw the huge teddy bear she'd chosen. "For me?" he inquired. "Or the baby?"

"It had your name on the tag, didn't it?" she responded, then grinned. "But I know you're the sort of man who'd want to share with his baby."

"We'll see," he said, settling the bear beside him in the crook of his arm. "I kind of like this guy. He snuggles up and doesn't talk back."

"Watch it," she warned, laughing.

Whether it was the gift's placement in the corner or Lizzy's unerring sense of the dramatic, Clint's present for Angela was the last one delivered. It took help from Justin to drag it across the room.

Angela stared from the huge box to Clint and back again. "What on earth?"

"You won't know until you open it," he teased.

She studied the package intently. "You didn't bring this home yesterday."

"Nope," he said complacently, amused by her perplexed expression.

"How'd it get here?"

"I had it delivered."

"From where?"

"Darlin', just open the thing."

"Yes," Harlan said. "Hurry up. We're all waiting to see what's inside."

Encouraged by everyone, she began enthusiastically tearing away the wrappings. As he'd instructed, though, the box was plain. It revealed absolutely nothing about the contents.

"Want some help?" he asked, moving to her side and taking his knife from his pocket. He opened it and cut through the tape that sealed the flaps, then sat back and waited for her reaction. The entire room had fallen silent, and all eyes were on Angela as she peered inside.

She lifted out sheets of recycled packing paper, one after another. Clint watched her face intently and knew the precise instant when she saw the gift.

"Oh, Clint," she whispered, eyes shining. "It's beautiful."

"What is it?" Harlan demanded, trying to peer over her shoulder. "Let me help."

He lifted out an exquisite hand-carved cradle and set it gently beside Angela. Made of cherry wood, it was intricately detailed and polished to a warm shine. A puff of yellow bedding with teddy bears lined it. Clint imagined that giant teddy bear Angela had given him standing watch over the cradle and his child. It was as if they'd been on the same wavelength in some way.

"Son, that's a mighty fine gift," Harlan said, clapping Clint on the back. "Mighty fine."

Just then Angela gasped and clutched her stomach.

"Baby?" Harlan asked, regarding her worriedly. "Are you OK?"

"Honey, what is it?" Jessie said, rushing over.

Clint hunkered down beside her. "Angel, what's going on?"

He didn't like the way she looked one bit. Her complexion was pale, her eyes stricken as she met his gaze.

"I could be wrong," she said, "but I have a feeling that cradle arrived in the nick of time."

Clint stared at her, his heart slamming against his ribs. "What are you saying?"

"Unless I'm very much mistaken, I am about to have a baby."

Chapter Thirteen

If she hadn't been quite so panicky, Angela might have been amused by the stunned reactions to her announcement. Clint went absolutely white. Her father and grandfather, normally the most unflappable men she knew, started barking orders, most of them contradictory.

Her normally calm mother finally shouted over the commotion. "Enough!"

Angela grinned as everyone fell silent and stared at her mother. No one in the room knew any better than Jessie about the unexpected arrival of a baby. She hunkered down beside Angela and smiled reassuringly.

"You OK?"

"Just surprised."

"It could be false labor," Kelly offered helpfully.

The suggestion was echoed by Janet and Melissa.

"Clint, why don't you get her a glass of chipped ice?" her mother suggested.

Visibly grateful at being given an assignment he could cope with, Clint practically raced from the room. He came back with a glass of chipped ice and two excited housekeepers. Maritza and Consuela arrived chattering in Spanish, aprons flapping and hands waving.

"Harlan, how are the roads?" her mother asked. "Can we get her to the hospital?"

"I'll check," he said promptly. "If not, I'll call the snowplow driver and have him clear the way ahead of us. I pay enough taxes to get a few special privileges."

Just then another pain ripped through Angela. She latched on to Clint's hand and cursed a blue streak. He stared at her in shock.

"Oh, don't look at me like that," she grumbled when she had caught her breath. "I swore I wasn't going to do this."

"Do what?" he asked.

"Have this baby close to Christmas, much less on Christmas Day. Good grief, we'll be celebrating everything at once. My birthday, Christmas, everything."

"You should have thought about that before you got pregnant when you did," her mother said dryly.

"I should have thought about a lot of things before I got pregnant," Angela said, then cried out with another pain.

"How close?" she asked, panting. "Damn, I knew

I shouldn't have ignored that backache during the night.''

"Three minutes," her mother replied. "Harlan, forget the hospital. She'll never make it. Let's get her into one of the bedrooms. Dani, you come, too."

"Me? Why me?" Dani asked, turning pale. She looked as if she wanted to flee.

"Just come, please," Jessie said.

When Clint had carried Angela upstairs and settled her into bed, her mother turned to the obviously wary Dani. "Honey, you've got the most experience delivering babies of anyone in this room."

Angela wasn't sure whose wail was louder, her own or her cousin's.

The last bit of color washed out of Dani's face. "Me? I've delivered litters of kittens. I've delivered puppies. I've even delivered baby bunnies. Under duress, I've even managed to help out with foals and calves, but I have never delivered a child," she protested. "I really, really don't think this is the time to start."

"I agree," Angela said emphatically. In fact, the very idea horrified her. It was ludicrous, insane, totally out of the question. Fortunately, Dani seemed just as appalled as she was. Surely her well-educated, professional cousin could make them see reason.

Sweat beaded on Angela's brow as her body was wracked with another labor pain. Panicked, she clutched Clint's hand and demanded, "Get me to a hospital, damn you. I am not having this baby with the help of a veterinarian, even if she is the smartest, nicest cousin on earth. The baby will wait, if I have to hold it in with both hands.''

"I don't know," Clint said worriedly. "He seems a little impatient to me. The roads are an icy mess. Snow's still coming down. You heard what your mother said. Maybe we'd better play it safe.''

Angie panted, trying to ease another pain. As soon as she had breath to spare she glared at him and at her cousin. "I want a real hospital and a real doctor. No offense, Dani.''

"None taken. Nothing would please me more than to accommodate you and turn you over to a real doctor," Dani said fervently. "Maybe Grandpa can get his helicopter pilot to swoop in and take you.''

"Not in this storm," Clint insisted. He squeezed Angie's hand. "Darlin', we have to be sensible.''

"You should have thought of that nine months ago," she declared. "That was the time for straight thinking and protection.''

Clint grinned. "Angel, that particular horse is already out of the barn. Let's deal with the crisis at hand, OK?''

"Maybe we should just get my father in here. He has more experience at delivering babies than any of you do. He brought me into this world.''

"I'm not sure how much help he would be," her mother retorted. "The last time I saw him, he was sitting in a chair with his head in his hands muttering something about history repeating itself.''

She gazed up and found Clint hovering a few feet away from the bed. He looked so worried and ill at ease that she would have shipped him off to join the others if she'd had the heart. Instead, she figured what he really needed was something to do.

Resigned to making the best of a lousy situation, she called out to him. "Clint?"

He was by her side in an instant. "What? Are you OK? What can I do?"

"Help me breathe," she said, thankful that she'd at least had the sense to take the Lamaze classes in Seattle before she'd left. Of course, the coach she'd planned on having was still in Seattle, too, but hopefully Clint would be a quick study.

"Here's the deal," she said, and explained what she needed him to do. The explanation took a long time because she kept having to stop for the increasingly severe pains.

After a particularly bad contraction, Clint said, "That's *it*. No more babies. I don't ever want to have to go through this again."

"You?" all three women protested in a chorus.

He grinned sheepishly. "Okay...Angela. I won't let *her* go through it again." He gazed at her mother worriedly. "Are you sure this is the sensible thing to do?"

"Sensible or not, we don't have a choice," she said, then looked to Dani, who'd just returned after finally conceding defeat and going off to scrub up for the impending delivery. "Do we?"

"Afraid not," Dani said irritably. "I'd say this Adams is about to make an entrance, like it or not. Aunt Jessie, can you find a blanket and some towels? Sterilize some scissors, too. And hurry, for goodness' sakes."

"Of course. I'll be right back." She feigned a scowl at Angela. "Don't you dare have this baby while I'm gone. I want to be right here when my grandbaby comes into this world."

"Then I think you'd better hurry," Angela said, her voice catching, then altering into a muffled scream. She didn't know a lot about the duration of labor. What she'd read said first babies tended to take a long time arriving. Hers didn't seem inclined to play by the rules. Typical of an Adams.

"Pant," Clint ordered. "Pay attention, darlin'. You remember the drill."

Fortunately she did recall there was more to it than panting. Since it was obvious everything else she'd just taught him had flown out the window. He watched her intently, then nodded. He grinned sheepishly when the pain had passed.

"Now I remember," he murmured.

With the next contraction, Dani murmured, "Here we go. Push, Angie. Do it," she said more sharply. "Push now."

"I am pushing, you lousy, no-good animal doc."

"Don't knock the help, kiddo, or Clint will find himself in my place."

"Be nice," he said hurriedly. "Dani's your best shot at getting this baby delivered with professional assistance."

"Oh, I think you could handle it, just as well as she could," Angela shot back. "How many calves and foals have you delivered?"

"A few."

"More than a few," she reminded him.

"Then get down here and take over," Dani pleaded. "I have absolutely no ego here. I'll take whatever help I can get."

Clint released her hand and was about to move when Angela latched on to it again and let out a shout that shook the rafters.

"Oh, my," Dani murmured. "Come on, Angie. Once more with feeling. That's it. Come on. Do it *now!*"

Angela felt as if her insides were being torn apart. Then suddenly, barely an hour after the severe pains had started, it was over. She tried to lift herself on her elbows. Clint was on his feet.

"My baby," she whispered urgently. "I don't hear anything. Dani?"

Just as panic was setting it, she heard a feeble cry, followed by a lusty wail.

"That's more like it," Dani said triumphantly. She took one of the towels that Jessie had brought in just that second and wrapped the baby. Her expression triumphant, she walked to the head of the bed.

"Angie, Clint, may I present your son."

"A boy?" Clint whispered, gazing awestruck at the chubby, red-faced newborn Dani placed in Angela's arms.

"Told you so," she said, her eyes filling with tears. "Oh, Clint, he's beautiful."

"Handsome," he corrected, grinning. "Boys are handsome."

"Not ours. He is absolutely beautiful."

"He is, sweetie," her mother said. She turned and

hugged Dani. "You were terrific. I'll never be able to thank you enough."

"We won't be able to thank you enough," Clint said.

"No problem," Dani said, then sank into a chair as if her legs had suddenly turned to water. "I don't ever, *ever* want to do anything like this again, do you hear me? I've never been so terrified of messing up in my entire life."

"Now she tells us," Angela teased.

She glanced at Clint. "I have an idea." She beckoned to him and whispered. Clint nodded.

Angela grinned. "OK, then. Don't fall apart now, Dani. Come here and officially meet your new godson," she said.

"Oh, sweetie, you don't have to do that," Dani said, but her eyes were bright with unshed tears. She rubbed the back of her fingers across the baby's soft cheek. "But I'm glad you did. Have you decided on a name?"

"I have," Angela said. "Clinton Daniel Adams."

"Brady," Clint amended, a determined scowl on his face. "Clinton Daniel Brady."

"Do you see a ring on my finger?" Angela asked, looking at her mother and her cousin. "Either one of you? Is there a ring here?"

The two women exchanged a look.

"Bye-bye," Dani said. "Glad to be of help."

"Call us if you need us," her mother said, brushing a kiss across her forehead. "You were great, sweetie."

"You're abandoning me?" she protested. "How can you do that? I just had a baby."

"Clint's here."

"Yes, but he has his own agenda at the moment. I want somebody who's on my side."

"We are," her mother insisted. "That's why we're going. You two need time alone with your baby."

It wasn't the prospect of being alone with her child that scared the daylights out of her. Clinton Daniel was the kind of miracle it would take a lifetime to study and appreciate.

No, what terrified her was the glint of pure cussedness she saw in Clint's eyes. He'd been possessive and determined enough before. Now there was no telling the lengths to which he'd go to claim his son.

For a long time after Dani and Jessie left Angela's bedroom, Clint couldn't form a coherent thought. He kept staring at the tiny infant, who was now wrapped in a huge yellow blanket. His son. Practically bald except for a few strands of soft blond fuzz, eyes as big as saucers staring solemnly back at him, a tiny pink bow of a mouth. He was in awe of him.

"Would you like to hold him?" Angela asked.

"I...um, I don't know," he said warily. "What if I do something wrong?"

"Are you planning to drop him on his head?"

He stared at her aghast. "Of course not."

"Then you'll do just fine," she said, holding the baby up in the air for Clint to take.

He gingerly accepted the baby and his tangle of

blanket. His gaze locked on his son's face as if he were mesmerized.

"Hi, kiddo," he said softly. Everything else in the room faded into the background as he concentrated on this tiny gift from God.

"I'm your dad," he said. "You and I, we're going to have a great time together. I have this little spread up in Montana and one day it's all going to be yours. I'm going to teach you every single thing I know about ranching."

"You might have to wait just a bit for that," Angela said dryly. "At least until he can walk."

"You're never too young to know that there's a plan and what your part in it will be," he insisted. "It makes a kid feel secure."

"You never had that, did you?" she asked.

He glanced at Angela, surprised by her accurate guesswork. "My mother did the best she could. Besides, the past's over and done with," he said, his gaze never straying from the beautiful face of his boy. "This child right here, he's the future. He's all that matters now."

"You can't build your whole world around a baby," Angela argued.

Something in her voice, a surprising hint of testiness, alerted him that her mood was rapidly disintegrating and that he was the cause of it. Suspecting he knew why, he glanced at her. "You OK?"

"Just peachy."

"Did I forget to mention how you fit into this future?" he inquired, giving her a lazy grin.

"Don't try to charm me, Clint Brady. All you care about, all you've ever cared about is your baby."

The accusation confirmed his own guesswork. Her feelings were hurt by what she perceived as his priorities. "That's not true, darlin'. You've just given me the most precious gift on God's earth and you will always have a place in my heart for that."

"I didn't have this baby to accommodate you," she grumbled, reaching for their son. Staking her own claim, he imagined. Clint reluctantly put the baby back into her arms. Her expression softened at once.

"He is precious, isn't he?" she whispered.

"He is, indeed, though I have a feeling you and I had better enjoy him while we can."

"Meaning?"

"I think I hear a thundering herd on the steps. My guess is we're about to have company. That boy's going to get passed around like a football."

"Over my dead body," she said, visibly tightening her embrace. "They can look, but nobody's getting this baby out of my arms today."

Before Clint could stake his own claim in what was becoming a knee-jerk reaction of possessiveness, there was a hard knock on the door, followed by a muffled burst of excited chatter. He supposed they might as well give in to the inevitable.

"You ready, angel?"

Her expression was clearly torn. "Not really," she said finally, "but I suppose it's only right to share on Christmas morning."

Clint opened the door and found Jessie trying to hold off the entire Adams clan.

"One at a time," she said forcefully. Then at a plaintive look from her husband and her father-in-law, she relented. "OK, two. Luke and Harlan, you can go in."

Clint grinned at her. "You think you can keep control of this mob by yourself?"

"You ever seen a mother bear protecting her cubs?" she retorted.

"I get the picture. Call if you need backup."

"You call if you can't budge those two men out of there in five minutes."

Clint went back into the room just in time to see Angela handing their son up to her grandfather.

"Your first great-grandbaby," she said.

As he cradled the infant, Harlan's expression was filled with the kind of fierce pride and tenderness that Clint had once longed to see in his own father's face. He thought he saw Luke surreptitiously wipe a tear from his cheek before he took his own turn holding the baby. This was the kind of tight-knit family, bound by love and respect, that he'd always wanted. If Angela would only say the word, he would be a part of it.

"How're you feeling?" Harlan asked her.

"Like I've been run over by a truck," Angela admitted. "But I've never been happier. He's perfect, isn't he?"

"The most beautiful baby boy I've ever seen," Harlan declared.

"Grandpa, you say that every time there's a new baby."

He winked at her. "But this time I mean it." He turned and held out a hand to Clint. "Congratulations, son. He's a fine-looking boy. He'll do the Adams name proud."

"With all due respect, sir, he's a Brady."

Harlan shot him a look of understanding. "Well, of course, he is. But he's an Adams, too, and we take pride in our own, no matter what name they carry." He turned back to Angela. "Now I don't want you fretting about not having this baby in a hospital. I've called the Doc and he'll be here in an hour or so to check him out. He'd already got his sled out to come to the open house, so he said he'd just start a little earlier."

"Thanks, Grandpa." She smiled at her father, who was totally absorbed in studying Clinton Daniel's perfect little face. "You know what, Daddy?"

Luke tore his gaze away from his first grandchild. "What, darlin'?"

"I'm glad I had him at home. Now I know what it must have been like for you and Mom."

Luke grinned. "Darlin', you don't know the half of it. Dani is the next best thing to an M.D., compared to me. She was also stone-cold sober. Your mama got a rotten bargain when she stumbled up to my doorstep that night."

Angela shook her head. "I don't think so. I think that's the night we really became a family, even if it did take you a while to accept the inevitable."

Luke put Clinton Daniel back in her arms, then

kissed her. "I love you, baby. Now your Grandpa and I had better get out of here before your mother comes in after us."

"Could you ask her to give us a second before she sends in the next round?" Clint asked. "There's something I need to say to Angela."

"No problem," Luke said, giving his shoulder a reassuring squeeze. "You just let Jessie know when you're ready for more company."

After Luke and Harlan had left, Clint sat down on the edge of the bed, hip to hip with the woman he wanted so badly to be his wife. He reached out and gently brushed a fingertip across his son's cheek. His skin was so soft, just like his mama's.

"Clint?"

Her expression was questioning. He looked directly into her eyes and for a moment he lost his train of thought. She could do that to him, rattle him so badly he'd be tongue-tied. He swallowed hard and tried to collect his thoughts.

"There's something I should have said before," he said eventually. His gaze strayed to the baby nestled in her arms, then back to her. "Thank you. Thank you for my son. Thank you for not giving him away, the way you threatened to do."

For an instant he thought he saw disappointment flicker in her eyes, but then it vanished.

"He's my son, too," she said quietly. "I know what I said in Montana. It was awful and it was cruel. I have no excuse, except that I was upset." She smiled, but it was clearly forced. "Just like you said, though, that was in the past. I can't change it. I just want you to know that I will always take very good care of him.''

"We will, angel. *We* will take very good care of him.''

"And just how are we going to do that with you in Montana and me in Texas?''

Clint wanted to declare flatly that she was going to marry him and come back to Montana with him, but the stubbornness he saw simmering in her eyes warned him off making that particular declaration.

"We'll work it out.''

"I will not have this child bounced back and forth between two states,'' she warned.

"Neither will I.''

"Which leaves us with what choice?''

"I haven't got all the details figured out just yet,'' he admitted.

"Well, do let me know when you think you have a plan,'' she snapped.

"Don't be sarcastic, darlin'.''

"Go tell Mother to let the others in,'' she said through clenched teeth.

"Are you upset, angel?'' he inquired sweetly, delighted with the reaction. If he could keep her stirred up and off-kilter just a little longer, maybe he could come up with a surefire way to get her to tumble straight into his arms.

"Upset? Me? Of course not.''

"Then relax your jaw before you grind all your teeth to nubs,'' he advised. "Your family will get the idea that you and I are having a little squabble on what should be the happiest day of our lives.''

"We aren't having a little squabble," she said. "I am trying very hard not to kill you."

"Shh," he whispered. "You don't want the baby to hear you saying a thing like that about his daddy."

She regarded him sourly. "My hunch is he'll hear a lot worse before all is said and done."

Clint turned away before she could catch him grinning. The new tactic was working very nicely, he thought, very nicely indeed.

Chapter Fourteen

Clint was sticking to her like a damned burr. He was about as annoying, too, Angela thought irritably.

Maybe if he'd looked at her once, really looked at *her,* she would have felt better. Instead, he couldn't seem to take his eyes off his son.

She told herself she was glad he was so enchanted with the baby, so taken with fatherhood, but it might have been nice if just once he'd kissed her or squeezed her hand or even run a fingertip across her skin the way he did across the baby's. Every time she witnessed that trembling, awestruck touch, she was so jealous she could spit. How pitiful was that?

She glanced up as he came into her room. His gaze skimmed across her, then aimed straight for the cradle beside the bed. When he realized it was empty, then and only then did his gaze settle on her.

"Where is he?"

"Grandpa's got him downstairs showing him off."

"Again? I thought most of the state was here yesterday for the open house. They got a look at him then."

"I'm not sure, but I think he's just showing Consuela and Maritza that he can already make the baby smile."

"Didn't your mother say that was just gas?"

"Try telling that to Grandpa. He's sure Clinton Daniel is very advanced for his age," Angela said with a grin. She waited for Clint to make up an excuse and go chasing after his son. Instead, he pulled a chair up beside her bed and sat down.

"How're you feeling, angel?"

"Better than I expected. I'd be downstairs myself, but everyone insists I should be resting. Another twenty-four hours of this and I'll be stir-crazy."

"Maybe you should be thankful there are a dozen people around who are eager to take the two a.m. feedings."

She regarded him skeptically. "Are you relieved?"

Clint grinned sheepishly. "No. I want to do it myself. I jump up the minute I hear him so much as whimper, and I run smack into a traffic jam outside your door."

Angela chuckled. "You'd think I'd have the inside track. After all, I am in the same room, but even if I get to him first, someone plucks him right out of my arms and tells me to get my rest."

"They wouldn't be able to do that if you were breast-feeding," Clint said thoughtfully.

Angela hadn't even had time to consider that. Too many people had been trying to take charge in typical Adams fashion.

"You know, you are absolutely right. Everything's happened so fast, I haven't been thinking straight." She glanced at her watch and saw that it was just about time for another feeding. "Will you go down and retrieve our son?"

His expression was so eager, she wanted to laugh.

"I'll be back in a heartbeat," he promised.

"Don't let anybody talk you out of this," she warned. "They'll try."

"I'll tell them I have my instructions," he promised. "Then I'll grab him and run like hell."

Angela wished like crazy that she could be there to watch Clint repossessing his son. Nobody stood in Clint Brady's way when he was after something.

Suddenly, though, her amusement faded. Would it be like that when he decided he wanted to take the baby away from her for good? That possibility slipped into her head when she least expected it. It had been frightening enough before the baby was born, but now that he was here, now that she'd held him in her arms, she wasn't sure she could bear the thought of losing him.

By the time she heard Clint coming in the door, tears were tracking down her cheeks. He was babbling nonsense to the baby so intently that he didn't notice at first that she was crying. When he did, he stopped dead and stared.

"Angel? What is it? What's wrong? Did something happen while I was gone?"

"My baby," she pleaded, holding up her arms. "Please, I have to hold him."

He gently placed the baby in her arms, then studied her with bemusement. "Darlin', are your hormones going wacky or is something else upsetting you?"

Unwilling to explain the fear that had suddenly overwhelmed her, she shook her head. "I'll be fine. Just leave me alone with the baby."

Clinton Daniel began to whimper. Nothing she tried seemed to soothe him, which sent more tears cascading down her cheeks. Obviously she didn't know the first thing about being a good mother. Clint wasn't blind. He would see that and use it against her. Even now he was scooping the baby up and rocking him gently. The baby quieted at once, more proof that Clint would be the better parent.

"Mind telling me what upset you?" Clint asked mildly.

"It's nothing. I'm fine," she said, blotting her tears with a tissue and fighting for composure. "Let me have him. He's fussy because he's hungry."

Clint studied her worriedly. "Are you sure? Maybe this isn't the time to change the routine."

"It's hardly a routine," she said testily. "He's only twenty-four hours old."

Clint ignored her and glanced at the baby. "He's asleep again," he said softly as he placed him in his cradle. When the baby was settled, he pulled the chair a little closer to the bed. "OK, angel, tell me what's been going on in that head of yours?"

She sniffed and cursed the combination of hormonal swings and genuine terror. "Nothing."

"Tell that to someone who'll buy it."

"Clint, just go away. I'm fine."

He studied her intently, then sighed. "You aren't, by any chance, panicking that I'm going to run off to Montana with the baby, are you?"

Alarmed that he could read her so easily, she tried to feign shock. "Why would you say that?"

"Wild guess."

"Well, you can just take your guesses and go fly a kite."

He nodded, but didn't budge. "That's a productive approach."

"Are you suddenly into soul baring?" she countered. "Since when?"

"Maybe I just wised up and realized it would be smart to put all the cards on the table so there'd be no room for misunderstandings."

"Did this epiphany happen overnight?"

He grinned at her sarcasm. "No, it's been coming on for a few days now."

"OK," she said agreeably. "You go first."

"I'm not the one with the attitude."

"Maybe not, but I have a feeling my attitude might improve if you just this once said what was really on your mind. Try it."

He squirmed uncomfortably and remained as tight-lipped as ever.

"It's not so easy when the shoe's on the other foot, is it?"

"No," he conceded. "OK, I will tell you what's on my mind."

Now that he'd made the commitment to open up, Angela got a queasy feeling in the pit of her stomach. Maybe this was a really bad way to go. Maybe she wasn't ready to hear what was going on in his head.

"I've been trying to figure out a solution to our dilemma," he said.

His response took the option of silence away from her. "Any luck?" she asked warily.

"OK...as I see it, we have three choices. Well, one of them really isn't an option, but I'll lay it on the table. We could get married, baptize our son and head back to Montana together," he suggested, ticking it off on his fingers as if it were as unimportant as an item on a grocery list.

"Or, two, we could go into court and fight over custody and wind up with some judge deciding which one of us gets to keep him. Or, three, I could leave him here with you, forget all about him and let you raise him as an Adams."

She knew with absolute certainty that this last wouldn't be an option he would ever consider. As for a custody fight, as painful as it would be, she might have gone for that if it hadn't been for the whole Hattie Jones debacle. If that came out, well, the outcome in court might very well be a toss-up. She couldn't take that chance and Clint knew it.

"Are you trying to blackmail me into marrying you?" she inquired.

"Of course not. If you have other options you'd like to throw out here, by all means go ahead."

She considered and dismissed a few that were so outrageous not even she could think of a credible way to explain them.

"OK, what if we just worked out our own custody arrangement and had a lawyer draw it up?" she suggested hopefully.

He shook his head. "Now, you see, here's where I have a problem with that. I want my son with me. I don't want him bouncing from state to state, especially now when he's just a baby."

"We could wait—"

"Until he's older? I don't think so. I'm not going to miss one single second of watching him grow up."

Nor was she. The path kept twisting right back to marriage, Angela realized. A loveless marriage. Well, loveless on his part, anyway. She might not trust him worth two hoots, but she loved him anyway, for reasons that would never make a lick of sense to her. She sighed.

"I'll think about it," she said eventually.

He nodded. "Don't take too long, angel. Time's running out."

At the warning, her temper flared. "Don't threaten me. I can always take the baby and run again. It took you eight months to find me this time. I'll make damned sure it takes longer next time."

Clint seemed startled by her threat and her vehemence. Then his gaze narrowed and his eyes darkened. "Now it seems to me that's how we got messed up in the first place, with you making wild threats and refusing to listen to reason. Don't even think about running again, angel. Something tells me this time I wouldn't be searching all alone."

"Meaning?"

"Meaning that your father and grandfather would be looking for you right alongside me."

"They'd never join forces with you," she protested, but without much conviction. They would and she knew it. Clinton Daniel was an Adams and they would never ignore his existence or do anything to keep his father—a man they clearly liked and respected—out of his life. Besides, tough as they were, they were also a couple of old romantics. They believed in happy endings. For some reason they had evidently gotten it into their heads that she and Clint belonged together.

She sighed. If only Clint felt the same, she thought wearily. If only they could recapture the emotions they had felt when they'd first met. Now, though, whatever feelings they had were colored by betrayal and fear and distrust. She wondered for the hundredth time if even love could overcome all that.

Clint had found the entire conversation with Angela about their future unsettling. As casually as he'd tried to introduce the subject of marriage, he'd been feeling anything but casual. If he'd been hoping for a sudden acknowledgment of the inevitable, though, he'd been sadly disappointed. She wasn't about to give him an inch. He did have her thinking, though, and that was something.

He gave himself until the first of the new year to

make good on his scheme for getting Angela to admit she loved him. After that, with her or without her, he was going to have to head back to Montana. The thought of leaving her or his son behind made his stomach churn. His plan had to work. He was counting on it.

After another two days of sly hints and devilish taunts, he concluded that he had to be losing his touch. Just when he was dead-on certain that Angie was weakening, that she'd say yes to a proposal, she slammed on the brakes and put enough distance between them to keep him in a constant state of frustrated arousal. The woman was driving him crazy. One thing was certain, a lifetime wouldn't be long enough for him to figure her out. Meantime the clock was ticking and he was fresh out of ideas.

He'd lain awake half the night trying to assess his progress. As near as he could tell, it pretty much added up to zero.

When he staggered downstairs at the crack of dawn for some of Maritza's potent, eye-opening coffee, he found Luke there ahead of him.

"You look like something the cat dragged in," Luke observed, his expression amused. "Coffee?"

"Please."

"Baby keep you awake?"

No, it wasn't his son who was responsible for his lack of sleep. It was the kid's stubborn mother. He shook his head.

"Angela, then?"

"Bingo."

"I don't want to meddle, but if you'd like to talk about it, I can certainly listen."

The only fathers Clint had ever known well were the ones in this family. Unless he'd very much misread them, meddling was their middle name. "Thanks, anyway, but I think I'd better handle this on my own."

Luke nodded and regarded him thoughtfully. "You told me when we first met that you intended to marry Angela. Is that still your intention?"

"Yes."

"Have you asked her?"

"I've asked her, I've told her, now I'm trying to torment her into it by avoiding the topic completely."

Luke grinned. "I'd say that's your best bet."

Clint regarded his prospective father-in-law hopefully. "Do you honestly think it'll work?"

"In this family, reverse psychology is about the only thing that does. From the time she was an itty-bitty thing, Angie has been dead-set on going her own way, just the way I did. She couldn't wait to get away from Adams territory so she could prove she was her own woman."

"But she came back."

Luke nodded. "Exactly my point. We just had to be patient and wait for her to realize this was where she belonged."

"And that took how long?"

"Six years," Luke admitted.

"I am not waiting six years to claim my son," Clint exploded. "Can you see me commuting from my ranch to here every blasted month just to get a look at them? How am I supposed to convince her of anything from hundreds of miles away?''

''Maybe your absence will do the convincing.''

''We were separated for seven months. You've been around since I caught up with her. Do you see any sign that she's mellowing?''

''Seven months is a drop in the bucket. Like I said, Angie's stubborn. We all are.'' He smiled. ''But I think she's worth waiting for, don't you?''

Clint muttered a curse. ''Yes,'' he conceded eventually, ''but I still think it's a lousy idea. She may decide she can get along without me just fine.''

''That is a risk,'' Luke agreed.

Clint shook his head. ''It's not one I'm willing to take.''

''I do have one other idea,'' Luke said, ''but I'm not sure how well it will sit with you.''

''Try me. I'm a desperate man.''

''You could come to work with me.''

Clint stared at him. ''Here? In Texas?''

Luke grinned. ''That is where my ranch is.''

Clint was shaking his head before the words were out of Luke's mouth. ''That's very kind of you, but no, I can't do that. My place is in Montana. I can't let it fall idle, and I can't expect my foreman to go on running it by himself forever.''

''Let him hire somebody to help, or let him buy you out.''

''Not a chance,'' Clint said vehemently. ''I've worked all my life to own a spread of my own. I'm not walking away from it.''

"If you marry Angie, my ranch would be yours one day, anyway."

"No," Clint said. "It would be hers. I appreciate your offer, but I can't accept it," he repeated.

"Don't be stubborn," Luke said impatiently. "One of you has to break this impasse."

"And you think I'm more likely to bend than she is?" he asked with reluctant amusement.

"Experience would suggest it," Luke concurred. "Just don't rule it out. It might be the bargaining chip you need."

"You're giving Clint bargaining chips?" Angela asked from the doorway. She was clearly exasperated with the pair of them. "Who's side are you on, anyway, Daddy?"

"Just trying to get you two off dead center," Luke said cheerfully. He stood up and dropped a kiss on his daughter's forehead. "Talk, darlin'. Nothing's solved by silence. I ought to know."

Angela sighed as he left, then shot a wary look at Clint. "Tell me about this bargaining chip."

"It's not an option," Clint said. "Are you sure you feel up to being downstairs?"

"If I'd had the baby in a hospital, they'd have kicked me out days ago. Obviously the greatest medical minds in the world don't regard childbirth as a debilitating illness."

"That isn't what I asked. Can't you ever give a straight answer?"

"My, my, you are testy this morning. Daddy must have struck a nerve."

"I could do without the dime-store psychology."

"There's a shrink in Los Pinos who charges more. Care to try her?"

"You know, angel, you are trying my patience."

She didn't appear worried about that. "So?"

"It's a very dangerous path to take," he warned.

"Really? What happens if I test your patience? Will you storm off to Montana?"

So that was her game. He regarded her with sudden amusement. "It's not going to work, angel."

"What?" she asked, her expression all innocence.

"I'm not going to blow a gasket and abandon you here, even though that appears to be what you'd like me to do. Nor are you going to goad me into a display of temper that will have your family taking your side against me."

"Oh, well," she said with a shrug. "It was worth a shot."

She began to load a plate up with waffles and fruit. When she would have skirted past him and taken a seat on the opposite side of the table, he snagged her hand. The gesture caught her off guard. It took only the slightest jerk to have her tumbling straight into his lap. He caught the precariously tilting plate in one hand and set it safely on the table. His other arm circled her waist and held her secure.

There was fire in her eyes, when he met her gaze.

"Clint Brady, don't you dare."

"Dare what?" he inquired lazily.

Color bloomed in her cheeks. "Whatever you were thinking of doing."

"I was thinking of doing this," he said quietly and

slanted his mouth over hers, swallowing yet another protest.

She gave a token shove at his chest, then sighed against him. Her mouth opened to his. When the tip of her tongue grazed his lips, he almost exploded. He'd meant to seduce her, meant to catch her by surprise with her defenses down and remind her of what they'd once had together.

Instead, she had twisted things around the way she had a habit of doing. He was the one off-kilter. He was the one who couldn't seem to catch his breath, whose blood was thundering through his veins.

Mystified by how she'd done it, he stared into eyes full of mischief, eyes that reminded him of Hattie.

Suddenly he tired of the game, all of it. Carefully he lifted Angie and set her in her own chair, then gave it a less than gentle shove to put a few inches of additional space between them.

She looked startled, then confused, then hurt. He pushed away from the table and stood, as anxious as she for once to put some distance between them.

"I'm going…" His voice trailed off. He didn't know where he was going or what he intended to do. He just had to get out of this room.

"Clint?" she whispered, her expression suddenly worried.

He didn't answer, because for the first time in his entire life he was at a loss for words.

Chapter Fifteen

A cold, empty feeling settled over Angela as she watched Clint walk away from her. He'd sounded so final when he'd said he was going, as if he'd given up, as if he might be leaving for good.

Well, that was what she wanted, wasn't it? It was what she'd prayed for, that he would go and leave her and her baby alone. What did they say? Be careful what you pray for, because it could come true.

She sat at the table staring at her cold waffle and unappetizing fruit and tried very hard to convince herself that it was best that he was heading back to Montana. If he couldn't love her back, then what was the point of prolonging this agony?

But no matter how hard she tried to convince herself to let him go, a part of her kept envisioning the loneliness of a future without him. Seattle had been awful enough with her nights filled with dreams of the man she'd left behind and her days just time to be gotten through.

At least in Seattle she had known somehow that he was still searching for her, and in some awful, perverse way that had been enough to keep her going. It had given her hope that he hadn't given up on her, that they would be together again someday.

OK, maybe she was a fool, maybe she didn't have a smidgen of sense, but she couldn't let him leave, not without telling him how she felt. If he still wanted to go, if he couldn't bring himself to ever trust her again, well, so be it. At least she would have tried. Not trying would doom her to a lifetime of what ifs.

She hurried to the stairs, cursing the fact that there were so many of them and that she was so darned stiff and sore. It seemed to take her forever to get to the top.

She rushed straight to Clint's room and knocked on his door. When he didn't answer, she ignored everything she'd ever been taught about privacy and threw the door open. He wasn't there. In fact, there was no sign of him at all. With her heart thudding dully, she peered into his closets and released a sigh when she saw that his clothes were still inside.

He hadn't left, then, but she was sure it was only a matter of time.

Where could he be, though? A smile touched her lips as she came up with the only logical answer. Closing his door gently behind her, she crossed the hall to her own room where she'd left a doting Consuela keeping an eye on the baby. She opened the door, then hesitated, immobilized by the scene before her.

Clint was there, in a rocker by the window, the baby cradled in his arms. Clinton Daniel looked so tiny against that massive chest, so tiny and so very safe and secure. The picture brought a lump to her throat.

Clint glanced up then and his gaze locked with hers. "Quiet, angel. I just got him to sleep."

She tiptoed across the room and sat on the edge of the bed. "How'd you get Consuela out of here?"

"I told her I was starving. She went to fix me a hearty breakfast."

Angela stared. "But you just ate."

He shrugged. "So, I'll eat again. I figured it was the safest bet for getting some time alone with my son."

Angela forced herself to keep a light note in her voice when she asked the question that had been plaguing her. "Are you saying goodbye?"

The question seemed to take him by surprise. He searched her face intently, then asked, "Would it matter to you if I was?"

She swallowed hard against the tide of vulnerability that washed over her just thinking about giving a truthful answer. There was no choice, though. She had promised herself she would deal with him honestly, something she should have done from the first.

"Yes," she said softly. "It would matter to me."

"Why, angel?"

This was it, then. It was time for the truth, the

whole truth and nothing but the truth. "Because I'm in love with you."

A knowing smile began at the corners of his mouth and spread. "Oh, really?"

She nodded.

"Say it again," he prodded. "Your father's said it. Your mother's said it. Even your uncle's told me that, but I want to hear it again from you."

"Look, dammit…"

He grinned. "That's more like it. You were sounding a little out of character there for a minute, all docile and sweet natured."

She regarded him ruefully. "I'm afraid I will never be docile."

"Thank goodness."

"But I will be honest, Clint. I swear to you that there will never be another lie between us." She searched his face, trying to gauge his reaction. "Is that enough?"

"Enough for what?"

"Enough to make you stay, enough for you to trust me again."

He sighed. "Angel, trust will always come hard for us. We got off to a rocky start on that score."

Her pulse seemed to slow at his dire prediction. It was her fault, too. The unforgettable, unforgivable Hattie Jones fiasco would always stand squarely between them.

"I see," she said, defeated.

He reached over and tucked a finger under her chin. "No, darlin', I don't think you do. Just because you have to work at something doesn't mean it's bad.

I've always worked for everything that's important to me. The way I see it, nothing's more important than our future. I'll do whatever it takes to see that we overcome every obstacle the past has put in front of us. What about you? Do you believe our family's worth fighting for?''

Angela blinked back tears. She tried to form an answer, but the words simply wouldn't come. Finally she just nodded.

"Was that a yes?" he asked.

"Yes," she said, then lifted her gaze to his. Tears blurred her vision, but her voice was firm when she repeated, "Yes."

He gave a nod of satisfaction, then grinned. "Angel, you never asked, but there's something I think you ought to know."

A fresh burst of trepidation had her heart skipping a beat. "What's that?"

"This isn't just about the baby. It never has been," he said quietly. "I do love you. I tried not to, but it was like trying not to breathe. If my arms weren't occupied at the moment, I'd show you just how much."

She grinned. "I could put the baby back in his cradle," she offered.

"And risk having him start fussing again? I don't think so."

Despite Clint's protests, she took the baby anyway and settled him into the beautiful cradle his father had bought for him. He didn't so much as stir.

"At least your son has his priorities straight," she

said, slipping onto Clint's lap. "Now let's work on yours."

"There's nothing wrong with my priorities," he grumbled, but he didn't complain when she feathered kisses across his forehead, then sought out his mouth.

Angela kissed him with all of the yearning and passion she'd been saving up during their months of separation. She could feel the hard ridge of his arousal beneath her hip and the thundering of his heart where her hand rested against his chest. His heat and the purely masculine scent of him surrounded her, carried her back to another time and another place when the two of them had been all that mattered.

"I do love you," she whispered against his lips.

"I know."

"Always did."

"I know."

She pulled back and scowled at him. "You don't know everything, Clint Brady."

"Maybe not, but I know the only things that matter. You and me, that boy of ours, family, ranching."

"See," she said triumphantly. "Your priorities are improving already."

"That's because I have such an outstanding teacher. Your motivational skills are excellent. Anytime you'd care to give me another lesson, I'm up for it."

"Maybe we'd better wait for our honeymoon for the lesson I have in mind."

His expression sobered. "Darlin', I'm not so sure

we can fit a honeymoon in just now. I've already been away too long."

She was sure he was prepared to offer a whole laundry list of reasons why their honeymoon would have to be postponed, so she silenced him with another slow, lingering kiss.

"On the other hand," he began, his voice husky.

"If you'd let me get a word in here," she said, "I think I have a solution."

"By all means."

"We could honeymoon in Montana. It's certainly the most romantic spot I've ever seen."

"You want to honeymoon on the ranch?"

"Why not?"

"For one thing it won't be much of a honeymoon with me working and the baby with us."

"Consuela can look after the baby and I can help you work."

"Darlin', far be it from me to turn down such a generous offer, but you do have a very strange notion of what a honeymoon ought to be."

"Maybe more people ought to start their marriages the way they intend to live them. Could be honeymoons just set up a lot of false expectations that get ruined when the day-to-day realities set in."

"An interesting philosophy, but won't you be disappointed years from now when our kids ask what we did on our honeymoon and all you can tell them is that we worked our ranch?"

She shook her head. "No, because that's how we're going to make it *our* ranch, with me doing my part from the beginning."

He still looked skeptical.

"I mean it, Clint. This is what I want."

"OK," he said eventually, "but on one condition."

"What's that?"

"For our fiftieth anniversary, when we've turned the ranch over to our kids, we go around the world. We will make love in every romantic spot you've ever dreamed about."

"The only romantic spot I've ever dreamed of is in your arms," she confessed.

"Then we're off to a good start, angel, because I'm never, ever letting you go."

It was amazing how many strings could be pulled when the Adams name was mentioned, Clint concluded as he watched White Pines being transformed into an indoor garden for a New Year's Day wedding. The same crowd that had shown up on Christmas Day, despite a blizzard, was scheduled to return today, despite the competition from football and New Year's Eve celebration hangovers.

A part of him felt guilty that he would be taking Angela and his son away from all this, but she had assured him over and over that Montana was where she truly wanted to be.

Luke had grumbled at the choice, but had finally agreed that he would send Consuela along with them to help with the baby for the first month, just as Angela had predicted he would. Since the housekeeper rarely let the boy out of her sight now, Clint wondered what would happen when the time came for her to return to Texas. What the heck. Maybe they could persuade her to stay.

He gazed into the mirror and tried to reconcile the image of the man in the tuxedo with Clint Brady. He was so spiffed up he hardly recognized the once-poor cowboy who'd never paid a lick of attention to his clothes, if the money could be better spent on feed for the cattle.

"You ready, son?" Luke called out.

Clint opened the door to his room and found his future father-in-law and Harlan pacing the hallway. They, too, seemed to be anxious to get out of these monkey suits and back into working clothes.

He met Harlan's gaze evenly. "Thank you, sir, for agreeing to be my best man."

"Son, nothing could have made me prouder. I know if your family'd been able to get here on such short notice, you'd have asked one of your brothers, but I'm glad to fill in."

"No," Clint said. "You deserve the honor. You've been more than fair to me from the minute we met. A lot of men in your position wouldn't have been. The same goes for you, Luke. I hope I'll never let you down."

"Just keep our gal happy," Harlan said. "That's all we ask."

"Did I hear someone mention me," Angela called out from behind her door.

"Don't you dare open that door, darlin'. It's bad luck for the groom to see the bride on their wedding day," Harlan said.

"According to family legend, that didn't stop you

and Janet from having a little chat before your ceremony. The way I remember it, you walked down the aisle together.''

"Don't live your life by my example, girl.''

She opened the door. "I can't think of a better one, Grandpa.''

Clint would have closed his eyes or turned away just because of the silly superstition, if he'd been able to. Instead, though, he couldn't seem to tear his gaze away from the lovely vision before him. She had opted for simplicity in a narrow dress of white velvet edged with satin. From the front it was as innocent and sedate as any bride's ought to be.

And then she turned and he caught sight of the back...what there was of it. A deep vee plunged practically to her waist, exposing an almost indecent amount of soft skin.

"Aren't you afraid you'll get cold?'' he asked wryly.

"Not if you're doing your job,'' she said tartly, and sashayed down the stairs ahead of them all.

So, he thought as he followed her, the mischievous Hattie lived, lurking somewhere inside his angel. It ought to make the next fifty years or so damned interesting.

Epilogue

Angela sorted through the stack of mail Clint had picked up in town and seized the pale yellow envelope from home. She'd been waiting for days for a long, chatty letter from her mother. After all those years she'd spent away, knowing nothing, she could no longer seem to get her fill of news now that she'd been there at Christmas. Phone calls satisfied some of her curiosity, but she liked receiving mail. She could hold it in her hands and practically feel the bond with her mother. She could read it over and over. And, of course, her mother always tucked in snapshots from the latest family gathering. There had been a huge Memorial Day barbecue just the week before.

Sure enough, there were three or four pictures from the celebration. The one of her parents stealing a kiss, thinking they were unobserved, no doubt, made her smile. Another of Grandpa Harlan flipping huge steaks on the grill and waving Janet away had her laughing out loud. He would never trust her when it came to cooking. He'd always said she could ruin a hard-boiled egg without half trying.

"A letter from your mom?" Clint asked, pausing beside her to drop a kiss on her forehead.

"With pictures," she said, displaying them for him. "I'll bet Dad didn't know anyone with a camera was nearby when he planted that kiss on Mom."

"I don't think he'd care," Clint said. "Personally, I love seeing the affection between them. I hope we still have that when we're old and gray."

"We'd better," Angela warned.

"Then let's stay in practice," Clint suggested. He sat in an over-stuffed chair by the fire and held out his arms. "Come here and read the letter to me."

She went to him eagerly and, after snuggling into his arms, she began to read:

"Dearest Angie,
We all loved the picture of baby Clint on the horse with his daddy. He's so big for five months, and he's the spitting image of his father. Quite the little cowboy. Please bring him to Texas soon so we can all fuss over him.

"Life goes on here. Everyone misses you. Sharon Lynn and Kyle Mason are definitely an item. She still credits you with getting them out of limbo and into each other's arms. After all those years in Dallas, Jenny has decided to come home and teach in Los Pinos. Harlan Patrick and Justin are already studying college catalogues and Janet swears Lizzy will never, ever go away to school, if what she hears about college campuses these days is true.

"I wish you could have been here for the Memorial Day festivities. Your grandfather was in his glory, but I must say I think he's slowing down just a bit. I worry about what will happen when we lose him. He's the glue that holds all of us together."

Angela glanced at the snapshot again and looked for the signs of aging her mother had seen. It seemed to her that her grandfather looked as robust as ever. She continued reading:

"Harlan is such a remarkable man, please do make sure your son has a chance to get to know him. Maybe we can all be together again this year at Christmas. Of course with no babies due, it will probably be boring.

"Whoops, almost forgot. We think that Dani has met *the* man. So far, though, she is being stubbornly resistant to the idea. Typical Adams, though in her case at least I understand what's behind her reluctance. Maybe, if you come, you can give her a push. Until then, much love,

Mom."

Angela sighed and folded the letter.

Clint regarded her sympathetically. "Homesick, huh?"

"I was so sure I would never, ever feel home-sick," she said. "I have everything I ever wanted right here. You, our son, a home."

"I could try to make you forget about it," he of-fered, his hand closing over her breast.

She grinned. "I'll bet you could, too."

His fingers stroked and teased until the images of home almost faded. Then he sighed.

"It's not working, is it? Your body's with me, but your heart is back in Texas."

"Afraid so."

"Then we'll go home," he said. "Christmas? Thanksgiving? You pick."

She regarded him speculatively. He seemed to be in an indulgent mood. "The Fourth of July is just around the corner," she suggested hopefully. "We could take a long weekend. Grandpa would send the plane."

"You know, Mrs. Brady, you have absolutely no patience."

"Sorry," she said without much real contrition in her voice.

"And I have absolutely no willpower when it comes to refusing you something you want. The Fourth it is. You call and I'll start supper."

She wound her arms around his neck instead. "How did I ever get so lucky?"

She lowered her head and kissed him. She began working the buttons on his shirt, then slid her hands inside over heated flesh and solid muscles. Clint moaned as her caresses became more and more insistent. When she reached for the snap on his jeans, he covered her hand with his and looked directly into her eyes.

"I thought you were anxious to make that call."

She shook her head. "It can wait. Some things definitely take priority."

Clint stood up then and shucked off his shirt and boots and jeans with an efficiency that still startled her. She grinned at him. "Afraid I'll change my mind?"

"Nope, just encouraging you to hurry up and get naked, too."

"Unlike you, I do think there are some things in life worth savoring. Stripping happens to be one of them. Why don't you just stretch out on the bed and I'll show you what I mean?"

"I don't think so," he said, already fiddling with the buttons on her blouse.

As clever as he was with his own, he fumbled with hers. She'd always found that endearing somehow, proof that she could rattle him when little else in life could. Once in a while a woman deserved to have an edge with a man.

He didn't wait for her to finish undressing before his hands were everywhere, caressing, probing, pleasuring. She was breathless long before they tumbled into bed together, straining toward a first climax before he even touched the moist, sensitive core of her. With a quick, skimming stroke, he sent her over the edge, then settled back to take his time and do it all over again.

Her breath was coming in ragged gasps, her body was slick with perspiration and fiery with need by the time he slipped inside her, filling her up, joining with her in a way that made her feel whole and never failed to amaze her.

His movements were slow, languorous, as if they had all the time in the world, when the rapidly spiraling of sensation inside her said otherwise. With his gaze fastened to hers, he seemed able to tell the precise instant when one more stroke would have been too much.

"Not yet, darlin'," he said and stilled inside her.

Frustration and need had her thrusting her hips up, searching for release, demanding it. If she could have, she would have flipped him onto his back and ridden him, exulting in the sensations that never failed to astound her.

But there was pure joy in this, too, in letting him control the pace, in delaying the sweet, sweet end for as long as possible. She settled back to wait, to prove that she could be patient when it counted, but one tiny movement of his hips, the touch of his lips closing over her breast pitched her right back to a physical intensity that was just shy of exquisite torture.

And again, he drew back. He touched a finger to her chin, stroked a thumb across her lips, drawing her attention. "I love you, angel."

"I love you."

He smiled at that, then rolled to his back without releasing her. "Why don't you have your wicked way with me, then?"

Settled intimately astride him, she said, "I thought that's what I was doing."

He linked his hands behind his head. "Not so's I noticed."

She laughed at the hint of challenge in his tone and the spark of pure mischief in his eyes. "Why, you low-down, rotten scoundrel," she muttered, tweaking the hairs on his chest until he yelped. She laved the same spot with her tongue and had his breath catching in his throat and all signs of teasing fading from his eyes.

When she began to move her hips, his gaze locked with hers.

"Now that's more like it, darlin'."

"I'm so glad you approve," she said, her voice husky.

And then she was lost again to sensation, to the rasp of his day-old beard against her skin, to the hitching sound of his breathing and the rush of his blood when she touched a finger to the pulse at the base of his neck. Then all she felt was the heat, his and hers, so much heat that she was sure they would be consumed by flames.

The slick friction of their bodies melding was as new and thrilling today as it had been on the night they met. Familiarity and commitment had only made it better, had only deepened the bond that was renewed each time they made love.

There was trust now, too, trust that would last beyond this moment, trust that would carry them through eternity. It had been slow in coming, but Angela felt it each time they looked into each other's eyes, each time they made love with an abandon that could only come with honesty and hard-won faith in what they had together.

"Come with me, angel," Clint whispered. "Come with me now."

Angela smiled as they reached the peak together, both of them rocked by shattering sensation.

She collapsed against his chest, breathing hard and feeling like a million bucks.

"I don't think I'll ever be able to move again," she said eventually.

"I'm afraid one of us is going to have to," Clint responded.

"Why?"

"Our son is calling. It's dinnertime. And he's clearly impatient."

Angela struggled to untangle herself from her husband and the sheets. "I guess I'm just going to have to teach that boy to cook."

"You might have to wait until he's old enough to reach the stove," Clint pointed out. He kissed the tip of her nose. "I'll cook. You call your parents and tell them we're coming home for the next big barbecue."

"Not home," Angela said, her hand on his cheek. "This is home. I'll tell them we're coming for a visit."

A slow smile spread across his face and lit his eyes. If she'd known how much it would mean to him to hear her say the word, she would have said it much sooner. Texas and White Pines would never be far from her thoughts. Her family would never be far from her heart. But this *was* home now. It always would be.

As for their son, though she vowed never to say as much to him, he was their littlest angel, the brightest one in the universe. He would grow up knowing how special he was, but she prayed he would never feel the inadvertent pressures of living up to expectations.

And this man, she thought in wonder, watching Clint as he retrieved his scattered clothes, he was far more than the father of her child. She could admit it now, to herself and to him. He was her heart and soul.

* * * * *

Be sure to watch for Dani's story in
NATURAL BORN TROUBLE, coming in
February from Silhouette Special Edition.

Take 4 bestselling love stories FREE

Plus get a FREE surprise gift!

As seen on TV!
Free Gift Offer

With a Free Gift proof-of-purchase from any Silhouette® book,
you can receive a beautiful cubic zirconia pendant.

This gorgeous marquise-shaped stone is a genuine cubic
zirconia—accented by an 18" gold tone necklace.

(Approximate retail value $19.95)

Send for yours today...
compliments of ▼ *Silhouette*®

To receive your free gift, a cubic zirconia pendant, send us one original proof-of-
purchase, photocopies not accepted, from the back of any Silhouette Romance™,
Silhouette Desire®, Silhouette Special Edition®, Silhouette Intimate Moments®
or Silhouette Yours Truly™ title available at your favorite retail outlet, together with
the Free Gift Certificate, plus a check or money order for $1.65 U.S./$2.15 CAN. (do
not send cash) to cover postage and handling, payable to Silhouette Free Gift Offer.
We will send you the specified gift. Allow 6 to 8 weeks for delivery. Offer good until
December 31, 1997, or while quantities last. Offer valid in the U.S. and Canada only.

Free Gift Certificate

Name: _____

Address: _____

City: _____ State/Province: _____ Zip/Postal Code: _____

Mail this certificate, one proof-of-purchase and a check or money order for postage
and handling to: SILHOUETTE FREE GIFT OFFER 1997. In the U.S.: 3010 Walden
Avenue, P.O. Box 9077, Buffalo NY 14269-9077. In Canada: P.O. Box 613, Fort Erie,
Ontario L2Z 5X3.

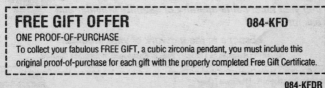

FREE GIFT OFFER
084-KFD

ONE PROOF-OF-PURCHASE

To collect your fabulous FREE GIFT, a cubic zirconia pendant, you must include this
original proof-of-purchase for each gift with the properly completed Free Gift Certificate.

084-KFDR

CHRISTINE FLYNN

Continues the twelve-book series—36 HOURS—in December 1997 with Book Six

FATHER AND CHILD REUNION

Eve Stuart was back, and Rio Redtree couldn't ignore the fact that her daughter bore his Native American features. So, Eve had broken his heart *and* kept him from his child! But this was no time for grudges, because his little girl and her mother, the woman he had never stopped—could never stop—loving, were in danger, and Rio would stop at nothing to protect *his* family.

For Rio and Eve and *all* the residents of Grand Springs, Colorado, the storm-induced blackout was just the beginning of 36 Hours that changed *everything!* You won't want to miss a single book.

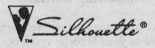

Available at your favorite retail outlet.

Welcome to the Towers!

In January
New York Times bestselling author

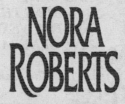

NORA ROBERTS

takes us to the fabulous Maine coast mansion
haunted by a generations-old secret and introduces
us to the fascinating family that lives there.

Mechanic Catherine "C.C." Calhoun and hotel magnate
Trenton St. James mix like axle grease and mineral
water—until they kiss. Efficient Amanda Calhoun finds
easygoing Sloan O'Riley insufferable—and irresistible.
And they all must race to solve the mystery
surrounding a priceless hidden emerald necklace.

Catherine and Amanda

THE Calhoun Women

**A special 2-in-1 edition containing
COURTING CATHERINE and A MAN FOR AMANDA.**

Look for the next installment of
THE CALHOUN WOMEN with Lilah and Suzanna's
stories, coming in March 1998.

Available at your favorite retail outlet.

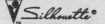